THE DOOR
in the FLOOR

Eddie seems a little awkward.
The whole house is much
wealthier, much bigger,
than his home.

"He wants a summer job."
—Ted
"With us?"—Marion
"Well, with me. He wants
to be a writer."—Ted
"But what would he do
with you?"—Marion

"There were also some beautiful things in the woods, and on the island, and in the lake. 'Why not take a chance?'" —Ted

"I read all your novels and all of your children's books. My favorite is The Door in the Floor.*"* —Eddie

"You're probably one of the few people on earth who read all my novels. What makes you think you want to be a writer, Eddie?" —Ted

"You can drive, can't you? I know boys your age—
you love to drive every chance you get." —Marion

"Timmy looks
guilty, but
Thomas looks
like—a wild
animal."
—Marion

"In the whole rest of your life, whenever you need to feel brave, just look at your scar. Your hand will grow bigger and your finger will grow bigger but the scar will always stay the same size." —Eddie

"I won't be a bad mother to her. I would rather be no mother than a bad mother to her." —Marion

"Mrs. Vaughn is
presently experiencing
the degraded phase."
—Marion

I'm just an entertainer
of children.
And I like to draw."
—Ted

"To put it simply, I need a ride home." —Ted

"Did you like my little surprise?" —Marion

"It's too hot. I hope
you'll forgive me
if I don't wear
the sweater."
—Marion

"She had a bad
dream. She said she
heard bangs, or
banging noises."
—Ted

This is the first time they have looked each other in the eyes for a long time. He leans in towards her. There seems to be something like a tender emotion between them, but it turns into something else.

Director, screenwriter Tod Williams on set

THE DOOR IN THE FLOOR

BALLANTINE BOOKS

New York

THE DOOR
IN THE FLOOR

A Screenplay

—

TOD WILLIAMS

A Ballantine Book
Published by The Random House Publishing Group

www.ballantinebooks.com

LIBRARY OF CONGRESS CONTROL NUMBER: 2004092613

ISBN 0-345-46900-3

Book design by Barbara M. Bachman

Frontispiece: Jeff Bridges

Manufactured in the United States of America
First Edition: June 2004
10 9 8 7 6 5 4 3 2 1

CONTENTS

—

INTRODUCTION

by JOHN IRVING

—

When I adapted my novel *The Cider House Rules* to a screenplay, the hardest part was compressing the passage of time. (In the novel, Homer Wells delays his return to the orphanage at St. Cloud's for fifteen years; in the film, Homer is away from the orphanage for barely more than a year.) I saw no way to make a movie of *A Widow for One Year*, because in the novel the feeling of the passage of time is as important as any major character.

Ruth Cole's story is told in three parts, each focusing on a critical time in her life. The first part takes place during the summer Ruth is four, when her mother leaves her and her father. (Ruth's mother, Marion, is grief-stricken over the deaths of Ruth's two older brothers. Marion is not just leaving her womanizing husband; she can't bear to love her daughter, Ruth, out of fear that she might lose her, too.)

The second window into Ruth's life opens when she is an unmarried thirty-six-year-old whose personal life is not nearly as successful as her literary career. She distrusts her judgment in men, for good reason. (Her father, Ted Cole, who is now seventy-seven, kills himself because he sees how his sexual lawlessness has influenced his daughter's sexual choices.)

A Widow for One Year closes when Ruth Cole is a forty-one-year-old widow and mother. She is about to fall in love for the first time. Her mother, Marion, who is now seventy-six, will reenter Ruth's life after a thirty-seven-year absence.

An impossible story structure to mimic in film. The passage of time resonates in many novels; it often enhances a reader's emotional attachment to the characters. Movies, for the most part, struggle with the passage of time, which often has the negative effect of distancing an audience from the characters.

I rejected several proposals for a film that began when Ruth was already a widow—the rest of the story would have been a flashback. The most emotionally affecting character in the novel is Ruth's mother, Marion; I did not want to marginalize Marion in a flashback. The most devastating part of the story (in the novel *and* the film) is the loss of Ted and Marion's sons; the death of those boys, from which Marion never recovers, makes her incapable of remaining in her daughter's life. I couldn't accept losing the premise of the novel in a flashback.

Then Tod Williams came along with his brilliant idea: make only the first part of the novel, up to when Marion leaves. Make Marion and Ted the main characters. (Ruth is just a child; she doesn't get to be the eponymous widow.) Make it a darker story—about the grief Marion can't get over, about how Ted hides his grief in philandering. Eddie O'Hare, the hapless writer's assistant to Ted—and Marion's sixteen-year-old lover—is, as he is described in the novel, a *pawn*.

I liked Williams's idea immediately. Nothing had to be compressed or lost; the film could be faithful to the first part of the novel. The rest of the novel remains intact for audiences who like the movie and want to know what happens to these characters.

This isn't a new idea. Volker Schlöndorff did it in his adaptation of Günter Grass's *The Tin Drum*. Schlöndorff made only part of the novel, up to the point when Oskar Matzerath starts to grow; when Oskar stops being a dwarf, the film is over. You want to know what happens? Read *The Tin Drum*. What a good idea!

Of course, we had to find another title. It was not possible to call the film *A Widow for One Year*—not when Ruth is only four at the end of the film, many years away from being a widow. Tod Williams, who is called Kip, wanted to use the title of one of Ted Cole's children's stories—the creepiest of them. In fact, *The Door in the Floor* is such a disturbing "children's story" that it has become a cult classic among college students. And what a good title for this film!

Not only is the story symbolic of the demons Ted Cole conjures for children; it also represents Ted's descent into loneliness, an alienation from which he can't, or won't, escape. At the end of the movie, when Ted lifts the trapdoor in the floor of his squash court and descends from sight, he is leaving this world.

I have told Kip that his screenplay is the most word-for-word faithful translation to film of any of the adaptations written from my novels—including my own adaptation of *The Cider House Rules*. That's true. But his choice, to make only the first third of the novel as a movie, has a radically altering effect. One I completely accept.

In the novel, my sympathy resides almost wholly with Marion; notwithstanding that she abandons her daughter, Marion has a *reason* to do anything she chooses. She is grieving; she cannot recover from the loss of her sons. But in the film, the story of what happened to those boys *and* Marion is told (on camera) by Ted. On film, the teller of the tale earns our sympathy. Besides, Marion has left—not only her husband and daughter, but also the movie. We end the film with Ted.

It isn't that Kim Basinger (Marion) is less sympathetic than Jeff Bridges (Ted); it is that the Kim Basinger character exits the stage and we finish the story with the Jeff Bridges character. He is the one we see descending into hell through that squash-court trapdoor.

The Door in the Floor is darker than *A Widow for One Year* because there is no redemption for the characters. (Marion doesn't get to come back; Ruth doesn't get to forgive her.) And the movie accentuates Ted and Marion's grief; it is an analysis of what we recover from, and what we don't.

Even when you don't have to lose much in an adaptation from book to screen, you always lose something. Screenwriters learn to compensate for what they've lost; they substitute something for what they've had to take away. In the novel *The Cider House Rules*, Fuzzy Stone, the orphan who dies of a chronic respiratory ailment, dies on

Homer's watch—before Homer leaves the orphanage. In the film, I kept Fuzzy alive longer; I let him die on Dr. Larch's watch, long after Homer has left St. Cloud's.

In an adaptation, you can't be too literally wedded to the novel; you have to take advantage of what a movie can do. Tod Williams does that—and not only because he chooses to end the film with Ted's descent through that door in the floor. In a more lighthearted moment in the screenplay, Williams invents a brand-new scene—something that was never in the novel—to compensate for the novel's lost humor. (You would be half right to call *A Widow for One Year* a comic novel; you'd be dead wrong to call *The Door in the Floor* a comedy.) The Abernathy joke is crucial—not only as a moment of awkwardness between Eddie and Marion, but as an indelible truth about their differences.

The black-and-white photographs of the dead sons are critical to Ruth's life. Those photos are her only means of knowing her brothers, and of comprehending their irreplaceability to her mother and father.

"It makes me sad to think about them," she tells her father.

"It makes me sad, too, Ruthie," Ted tells her.

"But Mommy's sadder," Ruth says. (She's right about that.)

It is a stunning choice on Williams's part to begin the movie with Ruth dragging the chair down the upstairs hall and climbing up onto it, to more closely examine one of those photos. "Dead means they're broken," Ruth says. "Tell me what dead is," she asks her father, a four-year-old's question.

The film gives us a sense of symmetry when, at the end, we see that upstairs hallway dotted with picture hooks—all but one of the photographs are gone. The sound, both before and after the music starts, is of that angry squash ball bouncing off the walls in Ted's court in the second story of his barn. I neither began nor ended the first part of the novel with the image of that sorrowful hall, but it is absolutely the best place to begin and end the movie. I told Kip early on that *The Door in the Floor* would never be a distinguished film if all he accomplished was to be literally faithful to my book: he had to do something more.

Tod Williams has been extremely faithful to my novel, but he has also made his own film.

This is excellent work.

For those readers familiar with the finished film, you will note that some of the dialogue is different; also, some scenes in the movie may not appear in the exact same sequence in which they were written. Kip and I saw no reason to indicate these discrepancies on the page. A shooting script is not supposed to be a faithful record of what was shot; that would be a mere facsimile of the film. Kip and I think that the differences between the shooting script and the finished film are interesting, and should be left intact; nor does this screenplay reflect how the movie was edited.

—John Irving

THE DOOR IN THE FLOOR

A SERIES OF BLACK AND WHITE PHOTOGRAPHS:

The common subject is two boys, obviously brothers. There are pictures of them at three and five, eight and ten, twelve and fourteen, fifteen and seventeen. They are very handsome boys; the older one, THOMAS, is darker and mischievous-looking, the younger one, TIMOTHY, is blond and seems shy. In some pictures the boys are posed with a beautiful woman, MARION, who is obviously their mother.

The pictures are vibrant and active. And we can hear, faintly, the SOUNDS OF THEIR SUBJECTS.

One shows a four-year-old Timothy with a bleeding knee, and Thomas trying to apply a bandage.

Another shows the boys as teenagers in full ice hockey gear on the ice, flanking their proud mother. Thomas has a hockey puck in his mouth.

The following dialogue plays over the photos. One voice (TED) is adult, slightly rough, with an educated East Coast accent. The other (RUTH) belongs to a four-year-old girl.

RUTH (V.O.)
Dead means they're broken.

TED (V.O.)
Well . . . their bodies are broken, yes.

RUTH (V.O.)
And they're under the ground?

TED   (V.O.)

Their bodies are, yes.

RUTH   (V.O.)

Tell me what dead is.

TED   (V.O.)

When you look at Thomas and Timothy in the photographs, do
you remember the stories of what they were doing?

RUTH   (V.O.)

Yes.

TED   (V.O.)

Well . . . Thomas and Timothy are alive in your imagination.

INT. CAR—NIGHT

The car is not moving. SNOW blows in through the SMASHED WIND-
SHIELD. The car is ripped open. Broken glass, snow, and blood are scattered
everywhere. Somehow the left turn signal is still TICKING.

Thomas sits in the driver's seat, his chest crushed by the steering wheel.
Blood runs from his nose and mouth, his eyes are open. He is seventeen and
dead.

From our P.O.V. in the right back seat we can't really see Timothy, but he
doesn't seem to be moving.

The only sounds are the HOWLING SNOW STORM and the incessant
TICKING of the turn signal.

EXT. COLE BACKYARD—DAY—EARLY SUMMER

We are close on the eyes of MARION COLE, a 39-year-old beautiful
woman. We recognize her from the pictures, though she seems slightly older.

Sometimes, the way she blinks or the way her hair blows in the wind, it almost seems as if she is in SLOW MOTION.

She is lying on a lawn chair, her eyes focused on something distant. She is in the backyard of her large and casually elegant house in the Hamptons.

INT. UPSTAIRS HALLWAY—LATE AFTERNOON

TED holds RUTH, wrapped in a towel. Ruth's wet blond locks curl into salty ringlets. Ted is about 45 years old, but still very fit. They are looking at the series of expensively framed and matted photographs that line the long hallway. From the window at the end of the hall, you can see the ocean about a mile distant.

RUTH
It makes me sad to think about them.

TED
It makes me sad, too, Ruthie.
He kisses her gently.

RUTH
But Mommy's sadder.

TED
Well . . . yes.

EXT. COLE BACKYARD—MOMENTS LATER

Marion is looking at Ruth, who stands in front of her wearing a bathing suit and holding a little plastic shovel. Ruth is talking to Marion, and we see, as Marion does, the little girl talking, but all we hear is the TICKING of the turn signal.

INT. TED'S WORKROOM—SAME

Ted is on the phone, looking out the window at Ruth and Marion. Marion sits up, just as Ruth gets bored and runs away. The room is spare and bright and there are sketches and art supplies scattered all over. A cot sits against one wall. Ted holds a high-school yearbook on his lap.

TED

Yes. Hold on.

Ted opens the yearbook to a specific page.

TED (CONT'D)

Does the boy have a driver's license?

MINTY

(loud enough that we can hear it through the phone)
Certainly he has his license!

Ted pulls his ear away from the phone, wincing.

EXT. COLE BACKYARD—AFTER SUNSET

Marion is still in the chair, almost in the same position. Behind them, in the brightly lit house, we can see Ruth and the NANNY. Marion looks up at Ted, who stands near her. Ted is holding a copy of the Exeter yearbook, with his finger marking a page. She yawns and stretches and sits up, putting her feet on the ground. Ted drapes a pink cardigan over her shoulders.

TED

It still gets cold at night.

MARION

Thanks.

Ted looks around the yard.

TED

Jesus, look at this yard. We should clear out some of these
straggly-looking flowerbeds.

Ted looks at Marion inquiringly, but she doesn't really respond.

TED (CONT'D)

And I want to put in a swimming pool.

MARION

Why?

TED

For Ruth, when she gets older. Something like the one we had in
Providence. They loved it.

MARION

Don't do that. It's better like it is. She likes to swim in the ocean.

TED

And the lawn should be more like an athletic field.

MARION

No.

*Marion looks at him, but he can't look at her. Ted sits down next to her,
opens the yearbook to page 178 and shows this to Marion.*

TED

Look at this picture.

Marion glances at it. Ted notes her reaction.

MARION (TOO CASUAL)

Why? Who is he?

TED

He wants a summer job.

MARION

With us?

TED

Well, with me. He wants to be a writer.

MARION

But what would he do with you?

TED

It's mainly for the experience, I suppose. I mean, if he thinks he
wants to be a writer, he should see how one works. He should see
. . . what it takes.

MARION

But what exactly would he do?

TED

Well . . . .

*Ted watches Marion. She's lost in thought, looking at a picture of EDDIE
running track in the yearbook. Ted watches her, and coldly sizes up her interest in Eddie. She traces her finger along the contour of Eddie's shoulder.*

TED (CONT'D)

I've been thinking—I want to try separating. For the summer.
Marion rubs her eyes, sleepily. A moment passes.

MARION

Okay.

TED   (WITH TENDERNESS)

I think we should try and see . . . if we might be happier apart.

She just nods. He pushes some hair out of her face.

MARION

Okay.

Ted seems a little surprised at her easy assent.

TED

Just temporarily.

They look at each other. There's nothing else to say.

EXT. COLE BACKYARD — MOMENTS LATER

Ted is gone. Marion looks down at the picture of Eddie caught in mid-stride.

EXT. EXETER CAMPUS — MORNING — PHOTOGRAPH

Eddie is running through the woods. He is running for the cross-country team. We follow him for a while; he just seems to go faster and faster, filled with youth and energy. Even though Eddie is sixteen and tall, he still looks like a young boy. Eddie runs through an ARCHED GATE.

INT. RENTAL APARTMENT — NIGHT

A black and white photograph of Thomas and Timothy standing underneath the same arched gate. This picture hangs in a strange, unfurnished little apartment. A few open cardboard boxes are scattered about. Marion is trying to set up the place by hanging a few photos. The little black and white TV is on and Marion is not really watching Ted being interviewed on an intimate, intellectual show like Charlie Rose. *Ted is talking brightly and with humility about his work as a famous author of children's books.*

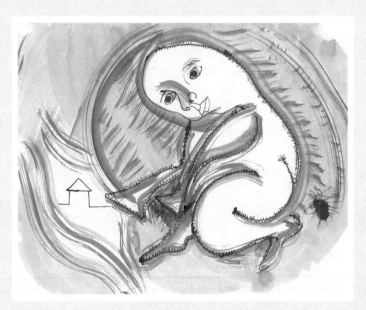

Drawing by Jeff Bridges

Drawing by Jeff Bridges

INTERVIEWER (ON TV)

...*The Door in the Floor*, a story about a male fetus who's not sure he wants to be born. One early reviewer said reading it to a child would be tantamount to abuse. Now it has something of a cult following . . .

TED (ON TV)

The Door in the Floor was the first book I wrote after the death of my sons.

Marion changes the channel to some inane show.

INT. EDDIE'S FAMILY HOUSE–NIGHT

Eddie and his parents, MINTY and DOROTHY, are gathered around the tube, which is tuned to the same show. Ted exudes charm.

Eddie is rapt. He is still wearing his workout gear but has a pen and paper to take notes.

INTERVIEWER (ON TV)

You began your career writing novels?

TED (ON TV)

Yes, but they were terrible novels. Unfortunately, I had to write three of them before I realized that I am not a writer of adult fiction. I'm just an entertainer of children. And I like to draw.

Eddie is trying to listen to Ted, but his parents talk right over the TV.

MINTY

Anyway, don't be nervous because he's famous. His sons were charming boys but mediocre students. They played a variety of the contact sports here at Exeter. They were both in my class, C plus/B minus I recall. They probably wouldn't have been accepted at Exeter if Ted wasn't an alumnus.

Drawing by Jeff Bridges

DOROTHY

He's been a *very* supportive alumnus.

MINTY

Without question. Although he was also a mediocre student. Ted
and I were in the same year, you know. We both chose the literary
life, he as an author, I as an academic. Anyway, just pick up what
you can, see if there's a method to his madness—that sort of thing.

INTERVIEWER   (ON TV)

. . . or why do cautionary tales for children come
so naturally to you?

TED   (ON TV)

Well . . . I think I can imagine their fears, and express them. In my
stories you can see what's coming, but you don't see *everything*
that's coming, I hope.
Eddie quickly jots this down, but continues to watch Ted closely.

INT. TELEVISION STUDIO—NIGHT

Ted sips his water.

INTERVIEWER

In my opinion, there is no better opening to any story
than the opening of *The Mouse Crawling Between the Walls*.
I mean the first line . . . .

TED

Tom woke up, but Tim did not.
Ted smiles.

Drawing by Jeff Bridges

INT. LIBRARY—NIGHT

A handsome black and white photo of Ted, smiling on the back of one of his books. Eddie is sitting, reading, wearing white cotton gloves. Eddie rubs his eyes, closes the book and then examines the photograph of Ted on the back flap. Ted looks as charming as ever.

INT. MASTER BEDROOM—NIGHT

Close on Ted's face. He is passed out, nude, snoring. The bedside table light is on. Ruth enters.

> RUTH
>
> Daddy. I had a dream. I heard a sound.
>
> *Ted opens an eye.*

> TED
>
> What sort of sound, Ruthie?

> RUTH
>
> It's in the house, but it's trying to be quiet.

> TED
>
> Let's go look for it, then. A sound that's trying to be quiet.
>
> *Ted gets up, still nude, and picks Ruth up and carries her out into the hall.*

INT. UPSTAIRS HALLWAY—NIGHT

They walk down the hallway that is lined with photographs.

TED

Come out, sound.

RUTH

Come out, sound!

TED

What did it sound like?

RUTH

It was a sound like someone trying not to make a sound.
Ted puts her down on the bed and pulls a pen and pad out of the night table drawer. Ted writes: It was a sound like someone trying not to make a sound. *Ted puts the paper between his teeth and picks Ruth up again.*

RUTH (CONT'D)

Your penis looks funny.

TED

My penis *is* funny.
Ted carries Ruth back through the adjoining bathroom. He stops in front of a picture of Thomas and Timothy. In the picture, Thomas is Ruth's age and Timothy is two.

TED (CONT'D)

I'll tell you a story about a sound. One night, when
Thomas was your age, and Timothy was still in diapers,
Thomas heard a sound.

RUTH

Did they both wake up?

TED

Tom woke up, but Tim did not. It was the middle of the night.
Tom woke up his father and asked him, "Did you hear that

Drawing by Jeff Bridges

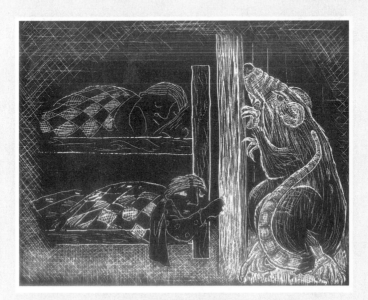

Drawing by Jeff Bridges

sound?" "What did it sound like?" his father asked. "It sounded like a monster with no arms and no legs, but it was trying to move," Tom said. "How could it move with no arms and no legs?" his father asked. "It slides on its fur," Tom said. "It pulls itself along with its teeth." "It has fur, and teeth, too!" his father exclaimed. "I told you—it's a monster," Tom said. "Let's go back to the room and listen for the sound," Tom's father said. *Ted walks with Ruth back into her bedroom and puts her in bed.*

TED (CONT'D)

It was a sound like someone pulling nails out of the floorboards under the bed. It was a sound like, in the closet, if one of Mommy's dresses came alive and it tried to climb down off the hanger. It was a sound like a ghost in the attic.

RUTH

What's an attic?

TED

It's a big room above all the bedrooms.
Ruth looks at her ceiling, concerned.

TED (CONT'D)

"There's the sound again!" Tom whispered to his father. "It's a monster!" Tom cried. This time, Tim woke up. "It's just a mouse, crawling between the walls," his father said. Tim screamed. He didn't know what a mouse was. It frightened him to think of something crawling between the walls. But Tom asked his father, "It's just a mouse?" His father thumped against the wall with his hand and they listened to the mouse scurrying away. "If it comes back again," he said to Tom and Tim, "just hit the wall." "A mouse crawling between the walls! That's all it was," Tom said. He quickly fell asleep, but Tim was awake the whole night long, because he wanted to be awake when the thing crawling between the walls came crawling back.

INT. LIBRARY—NIGHT

Eddie is reading along with the voice-over, and looking at the pictures.

TED   (V.O.)

Each time he thought he heard it, Tim hit the wall and the mouse scurried away—dragging its thick wet fur and its no arms and no legs with it.

INT. RUTH'S BEDROOM—NIGHT

TED

And that . . . .

RUTH

Is the end of the story.

Ted tucks her in. Somehow she doesn't seem comforted. Ted kisses her, picks up his piece of paper and stands up.

RUTH (CONT'D)

Where's Mommy?

TED

It's her turn at the other house tonight, remember? Tomorrow it's my turn, but she'll be here in the morning.

RUTH

Are there mice in this house?

TED

No, Ruthie. There's nothing crawling between our walls.

INT. RUTH'S BEDROOM—LATER

She can hear the sound of an IBM Selectric TYPEWRITER from the other room. And maybe the sound of something CRAWLING in the walls.

RUTH   (LOOKING AT THE CEILING, IN A WHISPER)
Attic . . . .

INT. RENTAL APARTMENT—NIGHT

Marion stands in front of the window, staring out at bugs swarming around a streetlight. The bugs become snow, snow falling past another streetlight. We hear the familiar TICKING.

INT. MINTY'S CAR—DAY

Close shot of a little, flashing, left-pointing arrow.
   But the arrow is in Minty's car. Minty is driving, or rather waiting to turn left. Eddie is trying to refold a map. Eddie's mother, Dorothy, sits in the back seat.

MINTY   (SMILING)
So, Edward, is this the pilot's error, or the navigator's?

EDDIE
Maybe you should navigate and I'll drive.

MINTY
So far your driving experience has been limited to Exeter, New Hampshire. I think it would be irresponsible of me to

thrust you prematurely into the driver's seat in an entirely new
state. Rhode Island and Connecticut each has their own
quirky rules of the road.

MINTY

EDDIE

What about New York?

MINTY

Oubliez cette idée, mon ami.

EDDIE

I might have to drive Mr. Cole places.

MINTY

Then I insist that you do some rigorous research on
the local traffic ordinances. Perhaps the library, perhaps the
Secretary of State's office. Perhaps New York State hosts
a web site on the subject.
*Minty pulls into a gas station and waves over the attendant, who leans in
Eddie's window.*

MINTY (CONT'D)   (TO THE ATTENDANT)

So how's this for a predicament? Here's a couple of lost Exonians
in search of the New London ferry for Orient Point.

ATTENDANT

You're in Rhode Island.

MINTY

The dulling of the mind is a terrible thing, Edward.

EDDIE

Yes, but nobody knows what an Exonian is, Dad.

EXT. FERRY DOCK–DAY

Eddie and his parents are saying goodbye. His mother pecks him on the cheek, his father shakes his hand solemnly. Eddie heads up the ramp to the ferry without looking back. Minty's eyes are wet with tears.

EXT. FERRY–LATER

The ferry is out in the middle of the Sound. It's a bright and windy day. Eddie stands at the rail, feeling a little queasy.

EXT. ORIENT POINT DOCK–DAY

Marion is waiting in her car. The world passes from shade to sun and back as the clouds slide overhead. Marion absentmindedly flips up the left turn signal. She watches the arrow blink and listens to the TICKING, until a BLAST from the ferry horn startles her. She turns off the blinker and climbs out of the car to watch the ferry dock.

EXT. FERRY–DAY

Eddie is having one last look at Ted's photo on the back of one of his books. He stuffs the book into his bag and disembarks. He's looking around for Ted, and though he sees Marion waving, he doesn't realize that she's waving at him.

She is so beautiful that she causes a MINOR COMMOTION wherever she goes.

Marion is right in front of Eddie but he still doesn't get it. He tries to walk around her.

MARION

Eddie.

Eddie stops suddenly and then looks at her confused. He is immediately smitten. She is very shaken and strongly affected by Eddie's resemblance to Thomas.

MARION (CONT'D)

Hello, Eddie. I thought you'd never see me.

EDDIE   (IN A WHISPER)

Mrs. Cole?

Both of them try but don't really succeed in regaining their composure.

MARION   (SMILING)

Marion.

They walk towards her dusty tomato-red Mercedes. Something about the way Eddie wrestles his suitcase makes her almost laugh a little. She seems more engaged now that he is here.

MARION (CONT'D)

Did you take the train to the ferry?

EDDIE

My parents drove me.

MARION

There's a train station right by the ferry docks, isn't there?

EDDIE

I don't know.

She stops walking and turns to look back at the ferry.

Drawing by Jeff Bridges

MARION

I think there is. I remember seeing it once, just to the right of the
main dock.

She looks at Eddie intently.

EDDIE

I'm sorry, I guess I should have noticed it.

She starts walking again. Eddie follows.

EDDIE (CONT'D)

I think your husband is a very great artist. I'm very excited to
work for him.

MARION

It will be interesting for you, I'm sure.
You can drive, can't you? I know boys your age—you love to drive
every chance you get.

EDDIE

Yes, ma'am. But I can't drive a stick yet.

MARION

It's automatic.

Marion tosses him the keys and walks to the passenger side.

EDDIE

Yes, ma'am.

MARION

Marion.

They get in the car.

INT. MERCEDES—DAY

Eddie starts the car.

EDDIE

I'm sorry about before. I was expecting Mr. Cole.

MARION

Ted lost his license three months ago. Anyway, you're not at
Exeter anymore. You can call us by our first names.

EDDIE

I don't know where we're going.

MARION

Just drive. I'll give you all the directions you need.

EXT. DRIVING SEQUENCE—DAY

The Mercedes slides through the landscape.

EXT. COLE'S HOUSE—DAY

*Eddie pulls the Mercedes into the driveway. Eddie gets out, and Marion
walks around and climbs into the driver's seat. Eddie is impressed by the
house.*

EDDIE

Aren't you coming in?

MARION

Not tonight.

Eddie tries to process this, but Marion doesn't offer anything more. Eddie retrieves his bags, and Marion pulls away. Eddie watches her go.

EXT. YARD—CONTINUOUS

Ted is chatting and saying goodbye to a sweaty squash partner, JOHN. He is attired in squash gear, eye protection and all, but looks relaxed. Ted comes across the yard to meet Eddie with a welcoming smile.

TED

Hey, Eddie. I'm Ted.

EDDIE   (VERY EXCITED)

It's an honor to meet you, sir. I want to thank you in advance for
this experience.

TED

Well, I hope you find it worthwhile.
(TURNING TO HIS SQUASH PARTNER)
John, this is Eddie. My new assistant.

JOHN

Hello.
They shake hands, briefly.

TED

See you next week.

JOHN

All right, ciao.
John heads out. Eddie turns to Ted.

EDDIE

I read all your novels and all of your children's books.
My favorite is *The Door in the Floor*.

TED

You're probably one of the few people on earth who read all my
novels. What makes you think you want to be a writer, Eddie?
Ted puts his hand on Eddie's shoulder and leads him towards the house.

EDDIE

Um . . . I wrote something. I brought it with me. I'd be extremely
honored if you might read it, whenever you aren't busy.

TED

Sure.

EDDIE

And my parents made me promise to get you to autograph our
family copy of *The Mouse Crawling Between the Walls*.

TED

Fine. Anyway, there's lots for you to do here.

EDDIE

What kind of things do you want me to do?

TED

Well—I'm sure there are lots of different tasks that will come up.
First, I need squid.
They go in.

INT. TED'S WORKROOM—CONTINUOUS

Ted cleans his hands. Eddie is taking notes. On the easel is a drawing of a woman and her son. Both the woman and the boy look like they are about to bite.

TED

I'm using squid ink for this book, and for all my sketches. There's a woman in Montauk, she's a fishmonger. She saves the squid ink for me.

EDDIE

Should I go today?

TED

Go tomorrow. If her husband is there, don't mention my name.
Ted rinses his head in the sink.

TED (CONT'D)

Also, I have to tell you, because it's a little confusing. You have arrived here during what is—a sad time—in a long and happy marriage. Marion and I have separated . . . temporarily . . . on a trial basis. We have rented a small apartment in town, and every other night one of us will stay there. During the day you'll work in the apartment, but your bedroom is here.
Ted whips off his sweaty shirt.

TED (CONT'D)

I know it seems unnecessarily complicated. It's hard to know what's best for our daughter. She's only four. It was the best idea we could come up with.
Ted pulls off his shorts and stands there in his jock-strap. Eddie looks away discreetly.

TED (CONT'D)

Anyway, your bedroom is up the stairs at the end of the hall.
Do you want to take your stuff up and relax
or unpack, or take a shower?

EDDIE

Unpack.

TED

Okay. Make yourself comfortable, Eddie.

EDDIE

Thank you, sir. I'm sorry about your marriage.

TED

Thanks, Eddie. Me, too. I'm sure you're going to do great here.
It will be a good summer for you and I'm glad to have you.
They shake hands.

EDDIE

Thanks.

INT. UPSTAIRS COLE HOUSE—DAY

*Eddie carries his wheeled suitcase up the stairs and finds himself in the long
hallway. Eddie examines the photographs.*

*Eddie walks along the hallway, examining the photographs, his suitcase
rolling behind him on the carpeted and bare sections of the floor. At the end of
the hall, Eddie tentatively opens a door.*

*From behind him, suddenly, comes a PIERCING SCREAM. He turns to
see Ruth staring at him. She SCREAMS again and runs away and down the
stairs. Somehow, Eddie has terrified her.*

Eddie ducks into his bedroom, and closes the door. It's a nice room. Eddie seems a little awkward. The whole house is much wealthier, much bigger, than his home.

He inspects his room. One photograph on the wall is of Thomas running track, almost an exact copy of the one of Eddie that Ted showed Marion. Thomas and Eddie look alike, as well.

Ted, dressed now, knocks and enters with Ruth in his arms. She is trying to hide her face.

TED

Sorry, Eddie. I wanted to introduce you to our daughter, Ruth.

EDDIE

Hello.

Ruth just stares.

TED

She thought you were a ghost.

EDDIE

I'm sorry.

TED

See, Ruth, it's just Eddie. He's very much alive. Right, Eddie?

Eddie nods, not very reassuringly.

TED (CONT'D)   (TO RUTH)

Okay?

She nods also, still wary. Ted and Ruth leave. Eddie sits on the bed.

INT. COLE KITCHEN—LATE AFTERNOON

Ruth and Eddie are eating grilled cheese sandwiches across from each other. ALICE, Ruth's day nanny, an 18-year-old young woman in a tube top and

short cut-off jeans, is sipping a Coke by the sink and flipping through a mag-
azine. Eddie tries not to eye her legs.

ALICE

Did you see the shrine?
She points at the ceiling. Eddie nods.

ALICE (CONT'D)
A little creepy, huh?

EDDIE

It's sad.

ALICE

You go to Exeter, right?

EDDIE

Uh-huh.
Ruth is looking at Eddie suspiciously.

ALICE

When I was in ninth grade I dated a senior from Exeter.

EDDIE

What was his name?
Ruth pulls his paper plate with half of his sandwich on it away from him.
Eddie isn't sure what to do. He's hungry but somehow intimidated by Ruth.

ALICE

Well, he's older than you, of course. His name was Chickie,
or Chuckie, or something.
He can't think of anything to say. She stares at him. Ruth pulls the ketchup
away.

EDDIE

Probably a nickname.

Alice just rolls her eyes. She wipes Ruth's face clean, clears the table, picks Ruth up, and leaves.

INT. RESTAURANT—NIGHT

Marion sits alone, eating dinner by herself. Her expression is absent. TICK-ING.

INT. COLE KITCHEN—NIGHT

Eddie sneaks into the kitchen, but doesn't turn on the light. He quietly pulls open the refrigerator and starts poking around. He thinks he hears someone coming and shuts the refrigerator quickly and quietly, but nobody is there.

The phone RINGS, startlingly. Eddie stares at it. It keeps RINGING. Eddie hesitates, then answers it.

EDDIE (ALMOST WHISPERING)

Hello? The Cole residence.

Pause.

EDDIE (CONT'D)

He's not here yet. Should I go look for him?

Pause.

EDDIE (CONT'D)

Unsteady?

Pause.

EDDIE (CONT'D)

Okay. Good night.

INT. VOLVO–NIGHT

Eddie is driving down a small lane. His headlights illuminate a bicyclist coming towards him. It is Ted. He looks drunk. Eddie slows to address him.

EDDIE

Um. Excuse me, Mr. Cole—

Ted pulls the bike over.

EDDIE (CONT'D)

Patrick from the Bobby Van's restaurant called and said you might—want a ride.

TED

I have a ride.

Eddie hesitates.

TED (CONT'D)

Go on home, Eddie.

EDDIE

Okay. Sorry . . . .

Ted rides on.

Eddie pulls away. He feels badly about disturbing Ted.

Ted watches Eddie drive off. On Ted's face we can see some black emotion.

He does a little figure eight to snap himself out of it.

DISSOLVE TO:

INT. FISHMONGER'S—MORNING

Close on ink being extracted from the guts of a SQUID and collected in a jam jar.

Eddie looks nauseous.

A large female fishmonger hands Eddie the jam jar with a lascivious smile and winks at him.

Eddie tries to smile back.

EXT. COLE DRIVEWAY—DAY

Eddie pulls into the driveway just as a large black Lincoln is doing the same. Eddie gets out of the Volvo and a small, semi-attractive woman dressed in black, MRS. VAUGHN, gets out of the other car.

> EDDIE
>
> Hi.

But the woman only glances at Eddie for a moment and marches haughtily around the side of the house. Eddie heads inside with his black jam jar.

INT. COLE KITCHEN—DAY

Eddie enters. Ted, wearing a bathrobe, is getting a snack out of the refrigerator.

> TED
>
> Great. You got it. Just in time.

> EDDIE
>
> Yes, sir.

Ted grabs an ice cube tray out of the freezer.

TED

Fine, pour it in here and freeze it. Otherwise it stinks like an
unwashed woman.

*Ted says this with a wink, and is satisfied to see Eddie blush. Eddie pours the
oily black ink carefully into the ice cube tray.*

EDDIE

What should I do now?

TED

I'm sketching with a model, so why don't you go
to the beach and take a swim.

EDDIE

I could straighten up the workroom—or something else.

Ted puts his arm around Eddie's shoulders and walks him to the door.

TED

No, that's okay.

EDDIE

Anything . . . really. I want to help.

TED   (WITH A SMILE)

No, you go ahead. Contemplating the waves will be a hell of a lot
more useful to you as a young writer than watching me draw.

EDDIE

Okay.

Ted nods and heads back to work.

EXT. SAG MAIN STREET—DAY

Eddie walks through the cemetery, looking at the old headstones, a towel slung over his shoulder.

He walks past a horse farm, where a girl and a horse are jumping over obstacles.

EXT. BEACH—CONTINUOUS

He arrives at the beach, kicks off his shoes and strips down. He sees Alice and Ruth. Alice is oiled and tanning, and Ruth is playing in the wet sand. Eddie waves at Alice, but she ignores him.

Eddie walks down the beach away from the crowd.

INT. TED'S WORKROOM—DAY

Ted is drawing Mrs. Vaughn. She is wearing her long skirt and a bra. He gets up to get a new pad of paper.

TED

Take off your skirt, please.

She looks at him, slightly concerned, but he reassures her with a big smile.

TED (CONT'D)

And your bra.

EXT. OCEAN—DAY

From overhead, we see Marion floating in the water. There are jellyfish nearby.

EXT. BEACH—DAY

Marion comes out of the water to find Eddie sitting on the sand. She comes over and stands next to him.

EDDIE   (SQUINTING UP AT HER)
You have—you have welts all over your—back—back and legs.

MARION
Jellyfish. Watch out for them.

EDDIE
Does it—hurt?

MARION
It hurts a lot.
They look at each other for a moment, until Eddie blushes and looks down. She walks away. Eddie gets up and walks with her.

EXT. BEACH ROAD—CONTINUOUS

They walk together, not too near each other, not talking. Eddie walks funny because there is gravel on the road. Marion notices this and sort of laughs a little.

EDDIE
My feet are still . . . soft from the winter.
Marion tosses her flip-flops to him.

MARION   (WITH A SMILE)
Wear mine.
He puts them on. They walk on.

EXT. BURGER STAND—NIGHT

Eddie rolls up in the Volvo to a burger stand where a dozen teen-aged kids are gathered. He goes to order his burger and notices that the girl behind the counter is Alice, the nanny.

EDDIE (SHY)

Hey, Alice. I didn't know you had two jobs.

ALICE

I have responsibilities. I'm not a kid anymore. What do you want?
Alice pours herself a soda.

EDDIE

Can I have a hamburger?

ALICE

Three twenty-five.
Eddie digs in his pockets, while Alice throws the burger on the grill.

ALICE (CONT'D)

Are you like a big fan of Ted's or something?

EDDIE

I think his books are masterpieces, in a way.
I think they are very moving.

ALICE

They're for kids, Eddie.

EDDIE

I know.

ALICE

Do you ever read books that don't have pictures?

EDDIE

Yes.

Alice puts his burger on a plate and places it on the counter.

ALICE

I wouldn't eat one of these burgers for a million dollars.
They're so gross.

A GUY WITH A BUZZ-CUT shoves Eddie out of the way and starts making out with Alice.

Eddie wanders over to a picnic table to eat his dinner.

INT. COLE HOUSE—NIGHT

Eddie walks quietly through the darkened house, and heads up the stairs. He stops on the landing as if he hears something, some muted whispering.

He continues up, cautiously, into the hallway, and sees Ruth standing on a chair, looking at the photos, talking to herself. She doesn't seem to notice him at first, then turns and looks at him. He heads to his room, and she returns to the photographs.

EXT. RENTAL APARTMENT—MORNING

Eddie pulls up and gets out of the Volvo. He is carrying Ted's notes and mail, and a Coke and a doughnut. He sees Marion's Mercedes parked in the driveway, so he sits on the hood of the Volvo to drink his Coke while he waits for her to come down.

EXT. RENTAL APARTMENT—LATER

Eddie is sort of napping on the hood, but he awakens to the sound of Marion coming out the apartment.

> MARION
>
> Good morning, Eddie.

> EDDIE
>
> Good morning, Ma'am.
> *They stand and look at each other.*

> EDDIE (CONT'D)
>
> Did you know that jellyfish kill more people
> every year than any other kind of animal?
> *Marion LAUGHS for the first time in a long time. Eddie smiles.*

> EDDIE (CONT'D)
>
> I looked it up.

> MARION
>
> I'll be more careful. And you shouldn't drink soda for breakfast.
> *She gets in her car and drives away. Eddie looks at his Coke, and then watches her go.*

INT. RENTAL APARTMENT—SAME

Eddie enters and puts his papers down on the little desk. He sniffs at the air. It smells like Marion. Eddie goes to the bed and holds the pillow to his nose, smelling Marion as hard as he can.

INT. RENTAL APARTMENT—DAY

Eddie sits at the desk and looks at Ted's scrawled notes. He feeds a blank sheet into the typewriter and we see what he transcribes: A Sound Like Someone Trying Not to Make a Sound. *He continues typing the story until the text fills about a quarter of one page. He's done for the day. Eddie sits still for a moment.*

He gets up and pokes around the apartment, opens a dresser and finds a few of Marion's clothes. He smells them. He carefully finds the crotch of a pair of panties and holds it to his face.

EXT. MOVIE THEATER—NIGHT

Marion's Mercedes is parked outside the theater. Eddie looks around, then goes to the ticket window.

INT. MOVIE THEATER—NIGHT

The movie is playing. Marion sits alone. Eddie watches the movie and watches her from a few rows back and over. Her pink cashmere cardigan glows in the light from the screen.

EXT. OUTSIDE MOVIE THEATER—NIGHT

Eddie walks out of the theater and nervously waits for Marion to emerge. He holds a bag of popcorn. We can tell from Eddie's face that it is a hot and muggy night.

MARION   (MILDLY SURPRISED)
Hey, Eddie.

EDDIE

Oh, hello, Mrs. Cole.

There's an awkward pause.

EDDIE (CONT'D)

Um. Did you just see that movie?

MARION

Yes.

EDDIE

How was it?

MARION

I don't know. Fine.

A group of teen-agers emerges from the theater, passing around them. Marion smiles.

MARION (CONT'D)

Is that your dinner?

EDDIE

Ummm. Sort of. I'm pretty tired of burgers. I've had one every
night since I got here.

MARION

So you bought your popcorn at the theater
but didn't see the movie?

EDDIE (CAUGHT)

Yes, uh-huh.

MARION

Ted doesn't get anything for you?

                                EDDIE
No, not really . . . I mean, he would, but I don't think Ruth likes
                            to eat with me.

                               MARION
I don't cook anymore, but I should take you to get something
healthy. I'm sure your parents wouldn't be too happy with us if
                     they knew how we're taking care of you.

                                EDDIE
              They wouldn't mind, really, I don't think.
                      They arrive at Marion's car.

                               MARION
Eddie? Would you let me take you to dinner sometime? I'll make
                  sure you get something decent to eat.

                                EDDIE
                                 Okay.
*Marion drives away. Eddie walks slowly back, looking over his shoulder to see
her go.*

                INT. UPSTAIRS HALLWAY—NIGHT

A formal photograph of the boys, 12 and 14, wearing suits.
                                                    DISSOLVE TO:

                  INT. RUTH'S BEDROOM—NIGHT

*The lights of a passing car wander across the ceiling. The nightlight is dim
and the room is dark. Ruth is lying in bed. She is awake and is listening to
SOFT GHOSTLY NOISES, like those two brothers might make.*

INT. EDDIE'S BATHROOM—NIGHT

Eddie is looking at a picture of Marion. She is about ten years younger, in a bedroom that looks like a fancy hotel room. It is morning, her hair is tousled and sunlight is streaming in. From under the blankets we can see a few extra small feet sticking out. Eddie's face betrays an overpowering feeling for Marion. Eddie tapes two little scraps of paper on the glass, covering the extra feet.

INT. EDDIE'S BEDROOM—SAME

Eddie has the picture propped up on the chair next to his bed. He is staring at Marion's beautiful face and beating off.
    Suddenly, there's a KNOCK at the door.

TED (OFF)

Eddie? Are you awake? I saw the light. May we come in?
Eddie leaps up and pulls on a pair of swim trunks, scrambling around. He returns the picture to its hook in the bathroom, but forgets to pull off the paper.

EDDIE

Coming!
Ted enters, carrying Ruth.

TED

Ruth wanted to be sure that one of the photographs was still here.
She gets very anxious when she can't see them, or if they get
moved. She gets upset if anything about them changes.

RUTH

There it is.

She points to another picture, where Timothy has skinned his knee and Thomas is holding a roll of gauze and demonstrating a clinical interest in Timothy's bloody knee.

RUTH (CONT'D)

He's just a little broken, but he's not going to die, right?

TED

Right.

RUTH

Not yet.

TED

Ruth had a dream.

Ruth sees past Eddie into the bathroom. She sees the pieces of paper on the other picture.

RUTH

Where are the feet?

Ted is moving towards the door with Ruth. Eddie slowly closes the bathroom door.

TED

What feet, Ruthie?

RUTH   (TO EDDIE)

What did you did? What happened to the feet?

TED

Ruthie, what are you talking about?

Ted is almost out the door, but Ruth is pointing at Eddie.

RUTH

Feet!

TED

I'm sorry, Eddie. We've gotten in the habit of showing Ruth these
photographs whenever she wants, and when we don't she really
gets worked up.

EDDIE

You can come see them any time.

TED

Say "Good night, Eddie"—okay, Ruthie?

RUTH   (TO HER FATHER)

What did he did?

They leave.

TED   (OFF)

It's not like you to be rude, Ruthie.

*Eddie bolts into the bathroom to remove the pieces of paper and scratches off
the remnants of the glue from the tape.*

EXT. RENTAL APARTMENT—MORNING

*Eddie arrives as usual, but there's another car there: the black Lincoln. Eddie
eyes it warily, but sits down to wait.*

*Ted comes out with Mrs. Vaughn. Ignoring Eddie completely, she gets in
her car and drives away. Ted spies Eddie and walks over to him. Eddie hands
him his coffee and doughnut.*

TED

Thanks, Eddie. Sleep well?

EDDIE

Yes, sir.

TED

Call me Ted. That was Mrs. Vaughn. She came over to discuss
some sketches.

EDDIE

Do you want me to drive you back home?

TED

No thanks, I'll walk. The revisions are on the desk.

EDDIE

Okay.

Ted starts walking away. Eddie heads up to the apartment.

INT. RENTAL APARTMENT—SAME

*Eddie walks in and puts his stuff down. He sniffs the air like he smells some-
thing not so good. The bed is rumpled and battered-looking. Eddie opens a
window.*

*He sits down at the desk and looks at the revisions. In the paragraph he
typed yesterday, one sentence has been cut. Eddie re-types the paragraph without the sentence.*

EXT. WORKROOM—DAY

*Eddie knocks on the exterior door. From inside, the sound of loud classical
music. Eddie knocks harder. Ted's hand appears, Eddie hands him the single
typed sheet. The door closes.*

EXT. BEACH—LATE AFTERNOON

Eddie is walking across the dunes towards the beach. He sees Marion on the beach and hides behind the dune to watch her. When she looks vaguely in his direction, he drops his face into the sand, and rolls over onto his back, looking at the sea grass and the sky, enraptured. Sand sticks to his cheek.

INT. RENTAL APARTMENT—MORNING

Eddie has Marion's clothes arranged on the bed. The bra is inside an unbuttoned blouse, the panties are the correct distance lower. Eddie is caressing the clothes as if Marion is in them. He is in masturbatory heaven, until he looks up and sees Marion standing in the doorway. She has arrived so silently that she is almost like an apparition. Eddie is frozen. Marion disappears from the doorway. Eddie is crushed, humiliated, destroyed.

INT. RENTAL APARTMENT STAIRCASE—
CONTINUOUS

Around the corner, Marion sits on the steps.

MARION
I'm sorry, Eddie. I should have knocked.

She can HEAR him, throwing clothes on and putting her stuff back in the dresser.

MARION (CONT'D)
Eddie, it's my fault. I'm not angry. I'm just embarrassed.

EDDIE   (FROM THE BEDROOM)
I'm embarrassed, too.

MARION

It's all right. It's natural. I know boys your age . . . .
Silence from the other room. Marion goes inside the apartment.

INT. RENTAL APARTMENT—CONTINUOUS

Marion stops at the door, and sees Eddie hanging his head in shame. She sits down on the little couch.

MARION

Come here—look at me.
Eddie is frozen, staring at his feet.

MARION (CONT'D)

Eddie, it's funny. Let's call it funny and leave it at that.
Marion smiles at Eddie.

MARION (CONT'D)

Eddie! Sit!
He sits on the couch with her.

MARION (CONT'D)

Eddie—I know boys your age. It's what boys your age do, isn't it?
Can you imagine not doing it?

EDDIE

No.
Eddie starts to tear up a little.

MARION

Eddie, listen to me. I thought it was one of Ted's women wearing
my clothes—I knew Ted wasn't touching them. Eddie, I'm

flattered. Really. It feels good to know that someone is at least *thinking* about me.
She's suddenly embarrassed again.

MARION (CONT'D)
I don't mean to assume you were thinking about *me*. Maybe it was just my clothes. I'm still flattered. You probably have lots of girls to think about.

EDDIE
I think about you! Only you!
He looks up at her with teary-eyed adoration.

MARION
Just think about my clothes. Clothes can't hurt you.

EDDIE
I think about what you were wearing when I met you.

MARION
I don't remember . . . .

EDDIE
A pink sweater—it buttons up the front.
She almost laughs.

MARION
That old thing? Really? Why?
Eddie takes this question seriously and takes a minute to think about it.

EDDIE
I mean, because of how your skin must feel against the sweater. I don't know how to say it.

MARION

That's okay—I get it. Sort of . . . .

Marion pulls the trash bag out of the kitchen garbage bin, and ties it up. Eddie stands. She hands the bag to him.

MARION (CONT'D)

Can you take that down with you?

EDDIE

Yes, Marion.

MARION

Not so serious, Eddie—not so serious.

Eddie exits.

EXT. BEACH—NIGHT

Eddie walks on the wet sand. A small crowd of young people, including Alice and her boyfriend, Buzz-cut, is gathered around a bonfire farther down the beach. Eddie watches from a distance, and then walks away.

EXT. ROUTE 27—MORNING

Eddie and Ted drive by in the Volvo.

INT. VOLVO—SAME

Eddie stops and waits to make a left turn.

TED

Don't turn your wheels in anticipation of the turn. If somebody rear-ends you, you'll be pushed into oncoming traffic.

EDDIE

Okay.

TED

Just a little tip.

EDDIE

Thanks.

They make the turn.

INT. VOLVO—DAY

Eddie pulls up to a huge, Meier-like house, with Ted in the passenger seat. MRS. VAUGHN, sexily dressed, opens the door and waits.

TED

I'll probably be about an hour. Why don't you look over the revisions?

Ted starts to climb out.

EDDIE

Do you want your supplies?

TED

Oh, yeah.

Eddie hands him the stuff. Eddie watches as Mrs. Vaughn leads Ted inside.

INT. VOLVO—LATER

Eddie still sits, waiting, bored. He looks at the revisions; two paragraphs of text.

INT. VOLVO–LATER STILL

Eddie is asleep. He wakes to Ted WHISTLING as he approaches. Ted climbs in.

EDDIE

Where's your stuff?

TED

Oh, I'll get it tomorrow.

Eddie starts the car. Ted WHISTLES more.

INT. RENTAL APARTMENT–NEXT MORNING

Eddie walks in with the mail and Ted's notes from the night before. He settles in and then gets up again and pokes his head into the bedroom. On the bed, Marion has arranged her pink cardigan and a pair of panties and a bra. Eddie gazes upon them in awe.

EXT. RENTAL APARTMENT–NIGHT

Eddie comes down wearing a blazer and a tie as Marion pulls up in the Mercedes.

MARION

Take off either the tie or the jacket. You don't need both.

Eddie unties the tie and hops into the car.

INT. RESTAURANT—NIGHT

Eddie and Marion are dining together. He wears the blazer. Marion is drinking wine. The restaurant is somewhat fancier than Eddie's used to, but he is eating industriously anyway.

MARION

Did you like my little surprise?
Eddie looks up, surprised again. He blushes.

EDDIE

Very much.
Marion laughs a little.

MARION

How's the work going for you?

EDDIE

I just re-type *A Sound Like Someone Trying Not to Make a Sound* every morning. Sometimes all he changes is a comma to a semi-colon, and the next day he changes it back. I don't get it.

MARION

Ted hired you because he needed a driver.
Marion considers Eddie for a moment and something stirs in her. She smiles. A waiter clears the table. After the waiter leaves . . . .

EDDIE

That's okay. I don't mind driving.

MARION

Boys your age are so sweet. My boys loved to help their father. During the summers Ted always had them running errands for

him, driving him around, working in the yard, but I think they
loved to help me the most.

EDDIE   (DEADLY SERIOUS)
I'll help you.

MARION   (SMILING)
Eddie, you're always so serious. Boys your age shouldn't be so
serious.

EDDIE
I know a joke, but it's not very good.

MARION
Tell me.

EDDIE   (TOTALLY DEADPAN)
There's this battleship out in the ocean, and the captain of it—
Captain Stern. Anyhow, this captain learns that the mother of one
of his sailors just died. The sailor's name is Midshipman
Abernathy. So the captain thinks and thinks and he tries to come
up with the best way to tell Abernathy that his mother died. This
captain, you know, he's a tough old bird, but he's still a generally
good guy. Finally, after staying up all night, he figures out a nice
way of telling him. The next morning he calls the entire crew up
on deck and says, "Gentlemen, all of you whose mothers are still
living step forward."
Eddie holds up his finger.

EDDIE (CONT'D)
"Not so fast, Abernathy."
*Eddie finishes the joke without a laugh and Marion smiles at him. The
waiter brings Eddie a huge hot fudge sundae.*

MARION

I like that joke, Eddie.

EDDIE

It's dumb.

MARION

Why don't you take Alice out on a date?

EDDIE

No way.

MARION

She's a nice girl.

EDDIE

She's not my type.

MARION

She's a good nanny, anyway. I think we were wrong to have had
Ruth. I hate that she has non-stop nannies. When we moved here,
the idea was a new place, a new child, a new life, I suppose. Ted is
a good father, but he doesn't know how to do a lot of the stuff you
have to do, and I can't . . . I can't with her.
Eddie is listening but at the same time devouring his hot fudge sundae.

MARION (CONT'D)

That's what I love about boys—no matter what, you just go on
about your business.

EXT. RESTAURANT—NIGHT

They walk towards the Mercedes. Marion hands Eddie the keys.

MARION

It's nice to be driven. Ted drinks at dinner, so I was always the
driver. Almost always . . . .

INT. RUTH'S BEDROOM—NIGHT

Marion and Eddie watch Ruth sleep. Marion holds a glass of white wine.

MARION

I used to be a good mother. I can't . . . .
*Marion walks out into the hall, and Eddie follows. They stop in front of one
of the pictures of the boys on a sailboat together.*

MARION (CONT'D)   (LOOKING AT THE PICTURE)
Do you ever think about death, Eddie?

EDDIE

No.

MARION

Do you ever have any regrets?
Eddie just looks at her. She notices his intensity, but turns back to the picture.

MARION (CONT'D)
I picked this one because they're in silhouette, and you can almost
imagine what they would look like now.
She moves to another picture. Eddie follows.

MARION (CONT'D)
Ted caught them sneaking down to peek at the Christmas
presents. Timmy looks guilty, but Thomas looks like—a wild
animal.
*They move to the next photo, in which Thomas is holding a flashlight and
they are looking at a basement trap door. Marion finishes her wine.*

MARION (CONT'D)

This one is funny because Timmy looks so . . . scared . . . .

She hands Eddie her glass and heads down the hall, into her bedroom, and shuts the door. Eddie stands still, moved.

INT. RENTAL APARTMENT—DAY

Eddie is passed out on the couch. Marion opens the door and enters. She is wearing sunglasses. Eddie sits up and tries to wake up. He has severe bed-head, and looks even younger than usual because he is sleepy.

MARION

I hope I'm not disturbing you.

She heads straight over to the picture she has hung in this room. Maybe she looks a little hung-over.

MARION (CONT'D)

You can tell in this picture, Timothy was more introspective—like you.

She wanders into the bedroom, and Eddie follows. Marion looks at another picture that she has hung in here. In the picture, her two sons stand under-neath an archway at Exeter. Above the archway there is an inscription: HVC VENITE PVERI VT VIRI SITIS.

MARION (CONT'D)

You know where this is, of course. What does it say?

EDDIE (TRANSLATING)

Come hither boys, and become men.

MARION

Come hither boys, and become men.
I put *this* one in here because I thought
it might remind you of home.

Marion notices her clothes laid out on the bed,
the pink cardigan with lilac underwear.

MARION (CONT'D)
Not pink with lilac.

EDDIE (BLUSHING)
I wasn't thinking about the colors.
Marion looks back at the picture of her boys.

MARION
I don't know if they had sex before . . . maybe Thomas had. He
was so . . . popular. But not Timothy—he was shy, and he was
only fifteen . . . . If a girl died before she had sex, I might say she
was lucky. But for a boy to die without . . . my goodness, it's all
boys want, isn't it? Boys and men. Isn't it true?
She looks at him, finally.

MARION (CONT'D)
It's all *you* want?

EDDIE
Yes. Before I die.

MARION
Have *you* had sex, Eddie?
He shakes his head. Marion takes two steps towards the bed, and slowly picks
up the panties that are laid out there.

MARION (CONT'D)
It's too hot. I hope you'll forgive me if I don't wear the sweater.
She pushes the cardigan aside and begins to undress.

MARION (CONT'D)   (WITH A LITTLE LAUGH)
Well, come on—take your clothes off!
Eddie stares.

MARION (CONT'D)
I can't do this alone.
Eddie undresses rapidly. Marion takes Eddie's hand and puts it between her legs. He comes.

MARION (CONT'D)
Goodness, that was fast.
They lay down together, looking into each other's eyes.

MARION (CONT'D)
Say it in Latin for me.

EDDIE
Huc venite pueri . . . .

MARION
Come hither boys . . . .
Marion gazes at the picture. In it, the boys look quiet for once.

EDDIE
Ut viri sitis.

MARION
And become men. But you still haven't had sex, have you?
Not really.

EDDIE
Not really. But I feel . . . complete.

MARION
I'll show you complete.
This time they fuck.

EXT. RENTAL APARTMENT—DUSK

Ted rides by on his bicycle and notices that both the Volvo that Eddie uses and Marion's red Mercedes are parked outside. He rides on.

INT. TED'S WORKROOM—DAY

Ted is sketching Mrs. Vaughn. She is naked, posed seductively and smiling tentatively. She is attractive, but Ted's sketch is horrible; it has a certain power, but is incredibly unflattering. His expression is dark and intense—he looks at her as if he is imagining what her corpse will eventually look like.

INT. TED'S WORKROOM—DAY

Ted is wiping his inky fingers with a rag. He spies Eddie in the yard, then dials a number on the phone.

TED
John, it's Ted. I have to cancel our game today.
Of course. Next week.
Ted hangs up and opens the side door. He calls to Eddie.

TED (CONT'D)
Eddie, are you finished with the rewrite? My squash partner just
cancelled on me. Do you want to play?

EXT. BARN—DAY

Ted and Eddie walk over to the barn carrying their squash racquets and dressed in athletic clothing.

Mrs. Vaughn staggers out of the workroom, too defeated to sneak. They walk past her through the yard.

TED

I converted the barn to a squash court
when we first bought the place.
It's not quite a regulation court in its dimensions, plus there's a
dead spot in the upper left hand side of the back wall. I'm the only
one who knows where the dead spot is, and I'm the only one who
knows the exact dimensions of the court. So basically,
I'm considered by even the best players on the island to be
unbeatable on my own court. By the way, you play much?

EDDIE

This is my third time.

TED

Too bad.

INT. SQUASH BARN—DAY

They climb up a narrow ladder.

INT. SQUASH BARN—LATER

Ted is both giving lessons to Eddie and destroying him.
At one point Eddie is blocking Ted's access to the front wall, but Ted takes
the shot and nails Eddie in the back with the ball.

EDDIE

Ow!

TED

You all right?

EDDIE

Yeah . . . .

TED   (CHUCKLING)

That was a good shot, though. It still made it to the back wall.

EDDIE

Isn't that a let? Aren't you supposed to just take a let
and not hit the guy?

TED

Technically, that's true. I'll take the let. Thanks.
Eddie has a welt. They play on. Ted pauses to instruct Eddie.

TED (CONT'D)

Where these red lines intersect, that is called the T. Whoever
controls the T controls the game. You need to win control of the
T before you can hope to win the game.
Ted scores a final point that Eddie runs into a wall trying to get.

TED (CONT'D)

That's the game.

Ted pats Eddie on the ass with his racquet.

TED (CONT'D)

You look like a boy who will sleep well tonight.

Eddie looks up, GASPING.

TED (CONT'D)

Maybe you need to catch up on your sleep anyway.

Eddie nervously tries to read Ted's remark, but Ted seems not to have meant anything special by it.

INT. RENTAL APARTMENT—DAY

Marion and Eddie are in bed together, fucking.

INT. BEDROOM—LATER

They lie together.

EDDIE

I was scared for a second yesterday. I thought Ted
maybe—maybe he knows.

She looks at him.

MARION

He wouldn't dare complain to me.

EDDIE

He might dare complain to me, though.

MARION

I have always been faithful to Ted.

EDDIE

Why didn't you leave him?
She thinks for a moment.

MARION

Ted understands me.

EDDIE

What do you mean?

MARION

Ted is the only person who really understands what happened to
me.
Eddie scratches his head, absentmindedly.

MARION (CONT'D)

You know who you just looked exactly like?
Eddie yawns.

MARION (CONT'D)

Hold on a second. I'll show you.
*She reaches over to a large stack of Exeter yearbooks and finds a picture of
Thomas fooling around at some social event.*

MARION (CONT'D)

You look just like him in this picture.

EDDIE

You have all the Exeter yearbooks?

MARION

The school sends them to us. Ted gives them lots of money. I know all about you. Last year you were on the Junior Debating Society and the Outing Club. This year you aren't.

EDDIE

I changed. I wanted to write for the *Pendulum*.

MARION

I know. I saw you looking . . . aloof among
a group of . . . here . . . .

She opens the current yearbook to the page. Eddie is sporting a dark shirt under his blazer.

MARION (CONT'D)

Timothy liked that look.

Eddie is propping his head up on one shoulder and looking along with her. He sneaks a glance at her.

MARION (CONT'D)

What kind of writing is in the *Pendulum*?

EDDIE

It's bad.

MARION

Don't be a writer, Eddie.

EDDIE

Why not?

MARION

Boys your age should stick to sports. Thomas and Timothy both played hockey. In the spring, Thomas played lacrosse and Timothy played tennis.

As she speaks, she shows Eddie photos of her boys from the older yearbooks. They are in virtually every candid shot, horsing around.

EDDIE
They're in lots of pictures.

MARION
Yes.

EDDIE
I'm not as popular, I guess.

MARION
Maybe you will be next year.

EDDIE
I'm not as good-looking, or outgoing.
Marion looks at him and ruffles his hair.

MARION
But you're cool, Eddie. And you're a good fuck.
Eddie likes this news, but tries to play it off.

INT. MASTER BEDROOM—EVENING

Ted is getting dressed in front of the mirror. He is wearing his interview outfit, and inserting cufflinks into the wrists of his shirt. He looks himself in the eyes—appreciative or probing? He dabs on some cologne.

EXT. COLE DRIVEWAY—EVENING

Eddie stands by the car, waiting, also dressed up. Ted checks out Eddie's threads, nods. They climb into the car.

INT. SMALL LECTURE HALL—EVENING

Ted is at the podium. The audience seems filled with young mothers. Slides of his illustrations are projected on a screen behind him. Eddie watches.

TED

There was a little boy who didn't know if he wanted to be born.
His mommy didn't know if she wanted him to be born, either.
This is because they lived in a cabin in the woods, on an island, in
a lake—and there was no one else around. And, in the cabin, there
was a door in the floor. The little boy was afraid of what was
under the door in the floor, and the mommy was afraid, too.
Once, long ago, other children had come to visit the cabin, for
Christmas, but the children had opened the door in the floor and
they had disappeared down the hole.
Eddie's eyes narrow as he understands this passage in a new way.

TED (CONT'D)

The mommy had tried to look for the children, but when she
opened the door in the floor, she heard such an awful sound that
her hair turned completely white, like the hair of a ghost. And the
mommy had also seen some horrible things. The things were so
horrible that you can only imagine them.
Eddie looks at the audience, and observes people's reactions.

TED (CONT'D)

And so the mommy wondered if she wanted to have a little boy—
especially because of everything that might be under the door in
the floor. Then she thought: "Why not? I'll just tell him not to
open the door in the floor!" But the little boy still didn't know if
he wanted to be born into a world where there was a door in the
floor, and no one else around. Yet there were also some beautiful
things in the woods, and on the island, and in the lake. "Why not

Drawing by Jeff Bridges

Drawing by Jeff Bridges

take a chance?" the little boy thought. And so he was born, and he was very happy. His mommy was happy again, too, although she told the boy at least once every day, "Don't you ever, not ever— never, never, never open the door in the floor!" But of course he was only a little boy. If you were that boy, wouldn't you want to open that door in the floor?

Ted finishes and smiles, and the audience applauds.

TED (CONT'D)

Every publisher thinks the illustrations are too rudimentary, and that there are too few of them. But I'm just an entertainer of *children*. And I like to draw.

He holds up his ink-stained fingers. Eddie rolls his eyes. Huge APPLAUSE as the audience is charmed by Ted's handsome humility.

INT. SMALL LECTURE HALL—LATER

Ted is finished. Women with questions and pens for autographs flock around him. A pretty woman with a young daughter fawns over Ted.

TED

Nudes are a requisite, fundamental exercise for anyone who draws. Like landscapes.

WOMAN

You don't prefer to use professional models?

Ted smiles reassuringly. Eddie waits, a step behind.

TED

Well, this is difficult to explain. If nakedness, I mean the feeling of nakedness, is what a nude must convey—well, there's no nakedness that compares to what it feels like to be naked in front of someone for the first time.

The woman smiles, shyly.

Drawing by Jeff Bridges

TED (CONT'D)
Right, Eddie?
Eddie, startled, nods vigorously, and then blushes.

INT. VOLVO—NIGHT

Eddie drives home, the lights from opposing cars in his eyes. He sneaks a peek over at Ted, warily. Ted might be asleep, but he isn't.

TED
I'm grateful to you, Eddie.

EDDIE
Why?

TED
I'm grateful to you for being such a good friend to Marion.
Eddie doesn't know how to take this.

TED (CONT'D)
She's been so unhappy. It's good to see her smiling again.
Ted is sincere.

INT. RENTAL APARTMENT—NIGHT

Eddie is fucking Marion. They're both sweating. He comes. He rolls off of her for a second, and looks up at the ceiling in a dazed way.

EDDIE
Thank you.
Marion shakes her head.

No. I'm selfish with you.

He turns back to her.

MARION (CONT'D)

Don't you need time to—recover?

Eddie shakes his head.

EXT. BEACH—DAY

Ruth, Marion, and Eddie have the beach to themselves.

Ruth is naked and playing with Eddie in the sand.

All three of them swim in the rough surf.

They sit together and dry off in the wind. Eddie and Marion surreptitiously hold hands.

Eddie finds a disposable camera in a beach bag and takes a picture of Marion and Ruth.

Marion seems more happy, and more loving towards Ruth, than we have ever seen her.

INT. UPSTAIRS HALLWAY—LATE NIGHT

Ruth is looking intensely at a picture of her brothers. She is standing on a chair. Ruth hears the SOUNDS of events depicted, sometimes fragments of their VOICES, sometimes more like SOUND EFFECTS.

She drags the chair from one picture to another. She seems very comfortable and sometimes even SPEAKS to the boys.

Ruth is nearer to the master bedroom now and she hears a noise she doesn't understand. It might be her mother crying or in pain. Ruth walks down the hall.

Ruth pushes the door, which is partially open, ajar.

INT. MASTER BEDROOM—NIGHT

From Eddie's point of view: he is fucking Marion from behind.

Eddie's face is radiant. Suddenly, he sees Ruth standing in the doorway, staring at them.

Eddie panics. He flies across the room, knocking over a lamp and grabbing a lamp shade to cover his hard-on. Marion sits down.

MARION (CALMLY)
Don't scream, honey. It's just Eddie and me.

RUTH
I thought it was Thomas.
Marion smiles reassuringly.

MARION
No, baby, it's just Eddie and me. Go back to bed.
Ruth quietly obeys. Eddie looks traumatized. Marion looks at him.

MARION (CONT'D)
That wasn't so bad, was it? Now we can stop worrying about that.

EXT. SAGAPONACK GENERAL STORE—NEXT DAY

Eddie climbs into the car and hands Ted his coffee.

INT. VOLVO—DAY

Eddie is driving Ted to Mrs. Vaughn's.

TED

Did you get the stamps?

EDDIE

Two rolls.

TED

Did they still have the ones with the nocturnal animals?

EDDIE

Yeah.

Ted takes a sip of his coffee, burns his tongue and reacts.

TED

Anyway, I presume it was Marion's mistake. But surely it *was* a
mistake for the two of you—to let Ruth see you together.

Eddie starts choking on his coffee.

TED (CONT'D)

I'm not threatening you, Eddie, but I must tell you that . . . you
may be called upon to testify.

Eddie doesn't understand.

EDDIE

Testify?

TED

In the event of a custody dispute, regarding which of us is more fit
as a parent. I would never let a child see me with another woman,
whereas Marion really has made no effort to protect Ruth from
seeing . . . what she saw. And if you were called upon to testify as
to what happened, I trust that you wouldn't lie—
not in a court of law.

*Eddie is silent. The tension in the car is thick. Ted sips his coffee, but Ted's tone
is casual.*

TED (CONT'D)

From the sound of it, it was a rear-entry position—not that I have
a personal problem with that, or with any other position, but for a
child I imagine that doing it doggishly must seem especially . . .
animalistic.

They pull up to Mrs. Vaughn's privet. Ted hops out.

TED (CONT'D)

I'll only be about twenty-five minutes today, just a quick sketch.

Ted shuts the door and heads up the drive. Eddie feels terrible. He almost feels
like crying.

EXT. BEACH–DAY

Marion, Ruth, and Eddie are at the beach. Ruth is playing with other chil-
dren.

MARION

He thought I would fight him for custody? I don't understand
how he could . . . I don't understand how he doesn't know me! I
thought at least he understood me.

Marion is furious and teary-eyed.

MARION (CONT'D)

I would never say that I'm a better parent than Ted! I would never
claim that! Even Ted is a better parent than I am!

Eddie is silent.

MARION (CONT'D)

Ted thinks that you're his pawn, Eddie.
But you're my pawn, not Ted's.

Eddie looks concerned.

MARION (CONT'D)
Aren't you?

He just nods.

INT. VAUGHN HOUSE—DAY

Ted is drawing Mrs. Vaughn, who sits before him, naked. The house is pristine. Ted is sketching furiously, and is covered in ink. CLASSICAL MUSIC is playing on the radio. He stands up and pushes her into a slightly different pose, and he leaves black marks from his inky hands on her face and shoulder where he touches her. She looks at him when he touches her, imploringly, but he doesn't notice. He just roughly yanks away a sheet that she is partially covering herself with, sits down and continues sketching.

INT. MASTER BEDROOM—NIGHT

Eddie and Marion are having sex, playfully, laughing.

INT. MASTER BEDROOM—NIGHT

Eddie and Marion lay together quietly, Eddie's head propped up on his hand. He gazes down at Marion with real love.

EDDIE
Tell me about the accident. I mean, do you know how it
happened? Was it anybody's fault?

She is frozen by his question. She turns away from him. He tries to comfort her, but she is gone. Her face is a mask, her body a stone.

EDDIE (CONT'D)
Marion? Marion?

He touches her, but removes his hand when she doesn't react.

EDDIE (CONT'D)

Mrs. Cole?

From the other room, Ruth calls.

RUTH   (OFF)

Mommy?

Marion doesn't even blink. Eddie shakes her—no response.

RUTH (CONT'D)   (OFF)

Mommy?

Eddie hustles into the bathroom and wraps a towel around his ass.

RUTH (CONT'D)   (OFF)

Eddie?

Eddie continues through the bathroom into Ruth's room.

INT. RUTH'S BEDROOM—NIGHT

Ruth is in bed.

EDDIE

Yes?

RUTH

Where's Mommy?

EDDIE

She's asleep.

RUTH

Oh. Did you take a bath?

EDDIE

Yes.

RUTH

Oh. But what did I dream about?

EDDIE

What did you dream about? Uh, I don't know. I didn't have your
dream. What did you dream about?

RUTH

Tell me!

EDDIE

But it's your dream.

RUTH

But what happened to the feet?

EDDIE

Nothing happened to them. Do you want to see them?
*She holds out her arms for him to pick her up. He carries her down the hall,
past the WHISPERING photos that only she seems to hear, and into his
bathroom.*
  The picture of Marion in bed in the fancy hotel room hangs in its place.

RUTH

It was early in the morning. Mommy was just waking up. Thomas
and Timothy crawled under the covers. Daddy took the picture in
France.

EDDIE

In Paris, yes.
Ruth points to the bigger foot.

RUTH

Thomas.
She points to the other, smaller foot and looks at Eddie.

EDDIE

Timothy.

RUTH

Right. But what did you did to the feet?

EDDIE

Maybe it never happened. Maybe it was a dream.

RUTH

No.

EDDIE

I guess it's a mystery.

RUTH

No. It was paper.

EDDIE

Don't you want to go back to bed?

RUTH

Yes, but bring the picture.

INT. RUTH'S BEDROOM—NIGHT

Ruth lays in bed, the picture propped up near her and lit by the night light.
The SOUNDS OF THE PICTURE are clearer than ever.

INT. MASTER BEDROOM—NIGHT

Eddie checks on Marion, but she still seems catatonic. He covers her and then goes to his own room. She stares into space with an expression of horror. We can hear the TICKING of the turn signal again.

INT. EDDIE'S BEDROOM—MORNING

Eddie wakes up to SCREAMING. It's Ruth's voice.

INT. BATHROOM—MORNING

There is blood all over the bathroom. It seems like Marion has slit her wrists, but then Eddie sees Marion and Ruth at the sink. Marion has a towel wrapped around Ruth's finger.

> MARION
>
> She cut her finger. She said it was glass. What glass, Ruth?

> RUTH
>
> The picture! The picture!

INT. RUTH'S BEDROOM—MORNING

The picture is on the floor. The glass is shattered. There is blood on the picture.

INT. BATHROOM—DAY

RUTH

Am I going to die?
This question strongly affects Marion.

MARION

No, you're not going to die!
She kisses Ruth.

MARION (CONT'D)

You're not going to die.

INT. DOCTOR'S OFFICE—DAY

Close on Ruth's finger getting stitched. She is crying loudly. Marion and Eddie stay with her.

INT. SQUASH BARN—DAY

Ted is with Eddie. Ted is slamming the ball against the wall, Eddie is not.

EDDIE

I put the picture in her room. It's my fault.

TED

That's not the point. The point is, you shouldn't have gone into her room in the first place—that's her mother's job.

EDDIE

I told you. Marion was asleep.

TED

I doubt it. I doubt that "asleep" would accurately describe
Marion's condition. I would guess she was zonked. She was a
zombie, wasn't she?

EXT. BEACH–DAY

Marion and Eddie stand in the shallow surf.

MARION

Did you tell him why?

EDDIE

No.

MARION

Tell him.
Marion is upset, and Eddie feels even worse.

EXT. COLE BACKYARD–DAY

*Ted is showering in the outdoor shower. He is soaping himself and rinsing as
he talks to Eddie.*

EDDIE

I did it to her. I asked her about the accident.

TED

It doesn't matter. She was a great mother to the boys,
but she's for shits now.

EDDIE

The whole thing is my fault.

TED

No, it's Marion's fault.

EXT. RENTAL APARTMENT—EVENING

Marion is walking quickly, Eddie follows her. They are near the apartment.

MARION

Who cares whose fault it is?

EDDIE

I care. I'm the one who let Ruth have the
photograph in her room.
Marion stops and turns to face Eddie.

MARION

This has nothing to do with you, Eddie!
She goes inside and leaves Eddie alone, thinking about what she just said.

INT. RUTH'S BEDROOM—NIGHT

Ruth wakes up from a nightmare.

INT. RUTH'S BEDROOM—A MOMENT LATER

Ted is trying to comfort Ruth, who is CRYING HARD and asking for her mother.

TED

I'm here, Ruthie.

RUTH

Mommy!

TED

Come on, honey.

RUTH

Mommy! Mommy!

INT. COLE KITCHEN—NIGHT

Ruth is still crying, and is still in Ted's arms. Ted is on the phone.

TED

Marion. Ruth wants you. Come here. I'll stay over there. She
won't stop crying. Okay.

INT. COLE KITCHEN—NIGHT

*Ted is holding Ruth, who is still upset when Eddie and Marion walk in. Eddie
tries to slide unnoticed into the living room.*

RUTH

Mommy!

Ted hands Ruth over to Marion.

MARION

What is it?

TED

She had a bad dream. She said she heard bangs, or banging noises.

MARION

What kind of banging noises?

Ted shakes his head.

TED

I don't know.

Marion carries Ruth out. Ted looks exhausted. Ted finds Eddie in the living room, trying to look innocuous.

TED (CONT'D)   (AS HE HEADS OUT TO THE CAR)

Eddie, drive me back.

EDDIE

Okay.

Eddie runs after him.

EXT. COLE DRIVEWAY—NIGHT

Ted and Eddie walk to the car. Ted can't help glaring at Eddie. They climb in, and when Eddie turns the car on the RADIO starts. It's playing some terrible POP SONG with lyrics that are explicitly sexual.

INT. VOLVO—NIGHT

They drive along, listening to the MUSIC. The lyrics are making Eddie uncomfortable. Eddie slowly and surreptitiously reaches for the knob to turn it off, but Ted stops him.

TED

Leave it, Goddamn it. I love this song.

They drive on. Ted taps his foot to the music awkwardly.

EXT. RENTAL APARTMENT—NIGHT

The car stops and Ted gets out without a word. Eddie pulls away.

INT. RENTAL APARTMENT—NIGHT

Ted stands over the mussed bed. The outlines of Eddie and Marion's bodies are clearly visible. There's a sexy bra on the nightstand.

INT. VOLVO—NIGHT

As Eddie drives back, the radio plays loudly. He seems very upset. His foot is heavy on the gas and the Volvo is going fast.

EXT. VOLVO—NIGHT

The Volvo zooms past.

INT. VOLVO—NIGHT

Eddie is trying to choke back his roiling emotions and doesn't seem to be paying attention to the road or to his speed. He wipes his eyes roughly as he rounds a turn and finds, in the middle of the road, several young adolescents on bicycles firing off Roman candles. Eddie SLAMS on the brakes and turns off the road, totally out of control. He TEARS into a potato field. The car is lost in a cloud of dust, and Eddie is shaken. The SONG on the radio ends and some COMMERCIAL starts playing. Eddie shuts off the radio and just sits in the car. As the dust settles, he can see the kids cycle away. Over the near horizon, July 4th FIREWORKS flash in the sky.

INT. RUTH'S BEDROOM—NIGHT

Marion sits on the edge of Ruth's bed and strokes her daughter's face lovingly. Ruth is soothed and her eyes slowly close. Marion lays down with Ruth, breathing her in. Marion's eyes slowly close, and her face relaxes.

Then Ruth strokes her mother's face.

INT. COLE KITCHEN—MORNING

Ruth and Marion are eating breakfast together and enjoying each other's company. Eddie walks in, rubbing his eyes. They both look at him. The phone rings. Marion reaches over and picks it up.

> MARION
> Hello?

INT. MRS. VAUGHN'S HOUSE—SAME

Mrs. Vaughn is surprised and doesn't say anything.

INT. COLE KITCHEN—SAME

Marion listens to Mrs. Vaughn's silence for a moment.

> MARION
> He's at the other house.
> *She hangs up.*

INT. MRS. VAUGHN'S HOUSE—SAME

Mrs. Vaughn holds the phone, flustered.

INT. COLE KITCHEN—SAME

MARION

He'll break up with her before Ruth gets her stitches out.

EDDIE

Before Friday?

MARION

I'll bet he breaks up with her today. Or at least he'll try. If she's
difficult about it, it may take him another couple of days. Summer
is the perfect length of time for one of his affairs.

EDDIE

The perfect length?

MARION   (NOT BITTER)

He starts with conventional portraits, often a mother with a child.
Then the mother alone, then nude. Then the nudes progress
through stages: innocence, modesty, degradation, shame.

EDDIE

Mrs. Vaughn—

MARION

Mrs. Vaughn is presently experiencing the degraded phase.

INT. KITCHEN—MORNING

Eddie, Marion, and Ruth are finishing breakfast. Marion is leafing through a packet of photographs from the one-hour developer. Alice enters.

ALICE

Good morning.

Marion is stuck on the photograph that Eddie took of her and Ruth. In the photograph they seem very loving towards one another.

EDDIE

I like that one of you.

Marion doesn't respond. The picture seems to confuse her. She looks up at Eddie.

MARION

What?

RUTH

Let me see!

EDDIE

I like that picture.

Marion just stuffs the picture back into the pack, opens a drawer and drops the pack inside.

MARION

Alice, I'll take Ruth today. You can have the day off.

ALICE

Are you sure?

MARION

Yes.

ALICE

I really don't mind . . . .

MARION

Thanks anyway.

EXT. BEACH—LATE AFTERNOON

Marion and Eddie sit in the sand, watching Ruth playing nearby. She looks
beautiful playing in the slanted sun.

EDDIE

Why now?

MARION

I have to . . . .

EDDIE

Why?

MARION

Because I don't know if I can stop myself—from falling in love.
Eddie's heart leaps in his chest. He looks at her quickly.

MARION (CONT'D)

With Ruth.
Eddie is slain.

MARION (CONT'D)

I can't love her. I won't. If I love her and something happens to
her . . . .

EDDIE

Nothing is going to happen to her.

Marion glares at him, wet-eyed.

MARION

I've stayed too long already.

Marion gets up and goes over to Ruth. Eddie feels like he is being strangled. He gets up and jogs away. He runs faster and faster. He stumbles in the sand, falls down, and looks back and sees Marion and Ruth far away. He gets up and runs on.

He heads down to where the sand is hard and wet, and runs a few steps before he notices thousands of tiny minnows flopping around on the sand. Eddie carefully picks his way out of the minnow area.

INT. MERCEDES—LATER

Eddie drives home. Marion holds Ruth on her lap, wrapped in a towel. Ruth looks up at her mother and Marion looks back. Ruth reaches up and touches Marion's face. Marion pulls Ruth into a tight embrace. Marion is trying to hold back tears.

MARION

I can't. I can't.

Eddie looks over at her. But she shakes her head at him.
Eddie looks back at the road, but sneaks glances at Marion and Ruth.

INT. RENTAL APARTMENT—NIGHT

Marion's on top of Eddie. She's fucking him and looking at the photo over the bed. She's crying, almost like she's in pain.

Eddie notices what she's looking at, and closes his eyes and turns his head away. Marion is looking intensely at the picture of her sons, tears pouring down her face freely. She is destroying herself.

INT. TED'S WORKROOM—DAY

Ted has gathered together over a hundred drawings of Mrs. Vaughn and is trying to close them into a large leather portfolio.

EDDIE

I'm going to do what?

TED

You're going to give her these, but not the portfolio. Just give her the drawings. I want the portfolio back.

EDDIE

Isn't she expecting you?

TED

Tell her I'm not coming, but that I wanted her to have the drawings.

Ted looks grave. Eddie looks worried. The drawings are quite horrible in the way that they show the sagging decay of the human nude.

EDDIE

It might be—awkward—to ask for the portfolio back.

TED

It won't be a problem.

EXT. MRS. VAUGHN'S HOUSE—DAY

Eddie slowly pulls into the driveway and stops the car.

INT. VOLVO—DAY

Eddie unpacks the portfolio. He can't help but see more and more images of Mrs. Vaughn's eviscerated body.

EXT. MRS. VAUGHN'S HOUSE—DAY

Eddie climbs out with his arms full of sketches and heads to the door.

Eddie RINGS the bell, but obviously Mrs. Vaughn saw him coming because she immediately opens the door. She's disarrayed. She is barely dressed in a bathrobe, her hair is wet, and she has white paste applied to her upper lip.

In fact, she resembles nothing so much as Ted's horrible drawings of her.

MRS. VAUGHN

What do you want? Where is he? Isn't he coming? What's wrong?

EDDIE

I don't know. But there are all these drawings . . . Can I put them down somewhere?

MRS. VAUGHN

Oh . . . the drawings . . . oh . . . .
She sort of stumbles back inside.

INT. MRS. VAUGHN'S HOUSE—DAY

Eddie follows her inside. The house looks like an art museum. Eddie carries the drawings to a gigantic dining room, and puts the stack down on the table. Mrs. Vaughn is right behind him.

MRS. VAUGHN

He's giving them to me? He doesn't want them?

EDDIE

He wanted you to have them.

She turns over the top drawing, a horrible nude. Neither of them can take their eyes off it.

MRS. VAUGHN

Oh . . . .

She turns it back over.

MRS. VAUGHN (CONT'D)

But when is he coming? He's coming Friday, isn't he? I have the whole day for him Friday. He knows I have the day, he knows!

Eddie is backing towards the door.

MRS. VAUGHN (CONT'D)

Stop! Is he coming Friday?

EDDIE

I don't know.

MRS. VAUGHN

Yes, you do know! Tell me!

She follows him outside.

EXT. MRS. VAUGHN'S HOUSE—DAY

The wind is ferocious. It blows open her robe, exposing her.

MRS. VAUGHN

Stop!

Eddie does.

MRS. VAUGHN (CONT'D)

Did he show you those drawings? Did you look at them?

Goddamn you! You looked at them, didn't you?

She comes out on the drive, picks up a small handful of pebbles, and throws them at Eddie. The wind SLAMS the door shut behind her.

MRS. VAUGHN (CONT'D)

My God! I'm locked out!

EDDIE

Isn't there another door that's unlocked?

They have to YELL over the WIND.

MRS. VAUGHN

I thought Ted was coming. He likes all the doors to be locked.

EDDIE

You don't hide a key somewhere for emergencies?

MRS. VAUGHN

The gardener has one, but I sent him home. Ted doesn't like the
gardener to be around. You'll have to break in.

EDDIE

Me?

MRS. VAUGHN

You know how, don't you? I don't know how to do it!

They're both upset now.

EXT. MRS. VAUGHN'S HOUSE—DAY

Around the side, by some French doors. Eddie takes off his T-shirt and wraps a rock in it. He swings the rock through a window, SMASHING the glass, and then carefully reaches his hand through to unlock the door. He opens it.

MRS. VAUGHN

You have to carry me over the glass. I have bare feet!

Eddie picks her up and carries her inside, with unconcealed disgust on his face.

MRS. VAUGHN (CONT'D)

How dare you—how dare you detest me?

He puts her down.

EDDIE

I have to go.

MRS. VAUGHN

You're not exactly living an unsordid life yourself—are you?

She grabs him by the wrist.

EDDIE

Please . . . I want to go home.

MRS. VAUGHN

Home!?

Eddie nods, and looks very teary. Mrs. Vaughn drags him by his wrist to the front door, opens it, and lets in a tremendous gust. Eddie runs to the Volvo, leaving his T-shirt behind him. Behind Mrs. Vaughn the cross draft blows the drawings all over the place, as if to torment her further.

INT. TED'S WORKROOM—DAY

Eddie hands Ted his portfolio, and stands there shirtless.

TED

Why did she think you looked at the drawings? Did you?

EDDIE

No.

TED

Christ! Of course you did.

EDDIE

She exposed herself to me.

TED

Jesus! She did what?

EDDIE

She didn't mean to, but she exposed herself.
It was the wind—it blew her robe open.

TED

Jesus Christ . . . .

EDDIE

She locked herself out because of you. She said you wanted all the
doors locked, and you didn't like the gardener to be around.

TED

She told you that? I can't spend the whole day with her Friday!
You have to come back and get me in forty-five minutes. Forget
that—in half an hour!

INT. RENTAL APARTMENT—AFTERNOON

*Marion is dressed, but Eddie is only wearing his tighey-whiteys. Marion
turns on the faucet and draws a glass of water.*

MARION

You have to trust me, Eddie.
On Friday morning you're going to leave him at Mrs. Vaughn's.

EDDIE

I know! For half an hour.

MARION

No, you're never going to go back. It'll take him most of the day
to get back home by himself. Something tells me Mrs. Vaughn
won't offer to drive him.

EDDIE

Ted's going to be really pissed off.

MARION

After you drive Ted to Mrs. Vaughn's, you're going to come back
here and get Ruth.

EDDIE

Why won't the nanny take her?

MARION

There won't be any nanny Friday. I need most of the day
at home alone.

Eddie wants to ask why, but doesn't.

EDDIE

The wind blew her robe open and I saw her. And then when I had
to pick her up, I noticed her smell—like on the pillows, only
stronger. It made me gag.

MARION

What did she smell like?

EDDIE

Like something dead.

MARION

Poor Mrs. Vaughn.

EXT. SAGAPONACK GENERAL STORE—MORNING

*Eddie and Ted come out of the store sipping coffee. There is a large moving
van parked near the store and several bored movers sit around the van; one
naps, one eats a donut. Eddie regards these movers nervously as he and Ted
walk to the car.*

TED

Wonder who's moving.

Eddie looks very nervous.

INT. VOLVO—MORNING

They drive away.

I read your story.

Eddie is surprised. Ted sips his coffee.

EDDIE

I thought you forgot.

TED

I just didn't have a chance to get to it before.

EDDIE

Not so good, is it?

TED

Well, it's very heartfelt. It's very personal. It seems like just
sort of a collection of personal anecdotes that don't really
add up to much.

Eddie is hurt but hides it.

EDDIE

I was just trying to see if I could write something
that seemed true.

TED

It seems true. It just isn't very interesting. It's sort of an emotional
outburst, but it isn't really a story. And the guy, Hank,
who dies at the end—well, you need to prepare the reader
for something like that.

EDDIE

I knew it, but it just didn't seem like the way things happen.

TED

You have to let your audience start guessing what's going to
happen, to start anticipating what's going to happen, and then you

surprise them, but you have to guide them through it.
You know what I mean?

EDDIE

Yes.

TED

Part of writing involves a certain manipulation, you see? It might
seem cold to you, but—it sort of is cold.

EDDIE

I guess.

TED

In fiction, everything is a tool. Pain, betrayal, even death.
These are like . . . different colors on a painter's palette . . . and
you have to use them.
Eddie just nods.

TED (CONT'D)

Also, the details could be more specific. Specific details create
entire scenes in the reader's mind. Not being specific—it's sloppy.
Sloppy thinking.

EDDIE

Specific details?

TED

Uh-huh. Smells, tastes, real details. But for a first effort . . . it's
really not *that* bad.
Ted pats Eddie on the shoulder affectionately.

EDDIE

Thanks.

TED

The prose is a little purple. A little pretentious.

EDDIE

Thanks, anyway.

TED

You're welcome.

EDDIE

Did you ever think about using a computer? It'd be easy to do
your own revisions that way.

TED

Maybe on the next book.

INT. VOLVO—MORNING

*Eddie drives and Ted sips his coffee. Eddie puts his coffee between his thighs,
and SIGNALS to turn onto Gin Lane. Now Ted starts to look nervous.*

TED

You better wait for me. I'm not going to last a half hour with that
woman. Twenty minutes, tops. Maybe ten . . . .

EXT. VAUGHN HOUSE—DAY

*Eddie pulls into the Vaughns' driveway on the CRUNCHY gravel, and puts
the car into neutral. They both notice tatters of paper scattered all over the
lawn, shreds of Ted's drawings.*

TED

Oh, boy.

A gardener, EDUARDO GOMEZ, stands on a ladder and pulls strips of paper out of the imposing privet. He pulls a large piece of paper that clearly shows an intimate piece of Mrs. Vaughn's anatomy down from a high piece of privet. He scowls at Ted, but they don't notice him.

There seem to be large wads of paper clogging the small fountain in the center of the driveway. Ted climbs out of the car and steps over to the fountain, which is near Eddie's side. The water has turned brown from the ink.

EDDIE

The squid ink.

Ted walks tentatively towards the house, his footsteps CRUNCHING LOUDLY on the pure white, pea-sized gravel. He calls back:

TED

Fi . . . five minutes!

Eddie stares out the windshield with a strange expression on his face as he puts the car into reverse and backs slowly away and out the drive. Ted can be seen dragging his feet up the front steps. Ted looks back as Eddie PEELS OUT. Ted is suddenly all alone.

INT. VOLVO—DAY

Eddie drives fast down Route 27.

EXT. COLE DRIVEWAY—DAY

Eddie gets out of the car and heads inside.

INT. LAUNDRY ROOM—DAY

Marion is wearing sunglasses. She's doing the laundry, and Eddie sits on the washer as Marion folds things from the dryer. Ruth is visible in the adjacent room.

> MARION
>
> When Ted asks you where I've gone, just say you don't know.

> EDDIE
>
> But where are you going?

> MARION
>
> You don't know. If Ted insists on a better answer, to anything, just say he'll be hearing from my lawyer. My lawyer will tell him everything. And if he hits you, just hit him back. He won't make a fist—at worst he'll slap you. But you should use your fist. Just punch him in the nose. If you punch him in the nose, he'll stop.
> *Eddie registers this.*

> MARION (CONT'D)
>
> You can call Alice if you need help with Ruth.

> EDDIE
>
> I don't like Alice.

> MARION
>
> You better get to like her a little. If Ted kicks you out, you're going to need a ride to the ferry at Orient Point.

> EDDIE   (ALMOST A WHISPER)
>
> Who's going to explain it to Ruth?
> *Marion just continues folding.*

MARION

I won't be a bad mother to her. I would rather be no mother than
a bad mother to her.

EDDIE

That doesn't make sense.

MARION

I don't want her to be like me. Like someone who would marry
Ted, like someone who would leave her daughter, like someone
who would fuck a boy like you.

EDDIE

Why not?

MARION

I'm contagious.

EDDIE

I don't understand.

MARION

What?

EDDIE

You.

MARION

Do you have to?
Eddie thinks, then shakes his head.

INT. COLE DRIVEWAY—DAY

The Volvo's doors are open. Eddie carries Ruth to the passenger side and puts her into her seat. Marion puts a bag of things for the beach in the back seat, and pulls a twenty-dollar bill out of her pocket.

MARION

You can take her anywhere for lunch. All she ever eats is a grilled cheese sandwich with french fries.

RUTH

And ketchup.

Eddie doesn't take the bill.

EDDIE

I have money.

Eddie leans in to buckle Ruth's seat belt and Marion slides the twenty into Eddie's back pocket. Marion then leans in towards Ruth.

MARION

Remember, honey. Don't cry when the doctor takes out the stitches. I promise it's not going to hurt.

RUTH

Can I keep the stitches to show you?

MARION

I suppose . . . .

Eddie and Marion stand and look at each other. Marion takes Eddie's hand and holds it to her breast.

EDDIE   (ALMOST INAUDIBLY)

I love you.

Marion turns and walks towards the house.

MARION

So long, Eddie.

Eddie walks over to the driver's side and climbs into the car. He looks out the rearview, hoping she'll look back. But before he starts the car Marion disappears into the house. Eddie looks down at his hand, which seems numb to him.

EXT. VAUGHN HOUSE—DAY

The spinning-sprinkler elegance is shattered as Ted comes tearing out of the house at full speed with Mrs. Vaughn chasing him. She is brandishing a large kitchen knife and SCREAMING. Ted gets the fountain between them. She tries to go one way, then the other.

MRS. VAUGHN

You are the—the—

TED

Wait!

She slashes the air uncontrollably with the knife.

MRS. VAUGHN

You are the—epitome of diabolism!!

Ted makes a break for the opening in the privet that leads to the street. Mrs. Vaughn is right after him.

From atop the ladder, Eduardo can see them running down the street away from town. Once in the open, Ted pulls away. Mrs. Vaughn gives up the chase a few driveways away, but throws the knife at Ted as he disappears into another huge privet bush.

INT. DOCTOR'S OFFICE—DAY

The doctor carefully removes Ruth's stitches. She is CRYING and YELLING. Eddie stands near.

EXT. GIN LANE—DAY

All is quiet again. Deep inside the privet, Ted looks at his watch. He looks hunted, muddy, and torn.

TED   (THINKING)
Where the hell is he? Marion is probably fucking his brains out.

INT. VOLVO—DAY

Eddie and Ruth drive. Ruth is okay now.

RUTH
Did we get the picture?

EDDIE
What picture?

RUTH
The feet!

EDDIE
Oh, the photograph . . . it's not ready.

RUTH
That's not very nice. My stitches are ready. My cut is all fixed up.

EDDIE

Yes, let's go to the frame shop and tell them to give us the picture.
Good idea.

EXT. GIN LANE—DAY

Ted emerges tentatively from the bush, all scratched and with branches stuck in his hair. He looks around both for Eddie and Mrs. Vaughn.

EXT. VAUGHN HOUSE—DAY

Eduardo, still atop the ladder, can see Ted come out and walk carefully back towards him. Eduardo looks around nervously.

As Ted creeps by the driveway, a silver Mercedes SUV tears out of the garage, SKIDDING on the gravel.

EDUARDO
Run!

EXT. GIN LANE—DAY

Ted hears Eduardo's warning, and starts sprinting. The SUV clips the ladder, leaving Eduardo stranded on top of the privet, and ROARS out onto Gin Lane.

The SUV is right on Ted's ass and about to flatten him when he makes a sharp right and rounds the corner.

Mrs. Vaughn immediately yanks her wheel right and turns onto Toylsome Lane, SPLINTERING the street sign as she cuts the corner.

Ted leaps into another privet.

EXT. TOYLSOME LANE—DAY

The SUV SCREECHES to a halt at the next intersection, waiting.

Ted crouches in a privet and watches, GASPING.

The SUV sits still, smoking, tail lights burning red, then slowly makes the turn away from Ted.

Ted stands up and hustles down the street in the opposite direction, back towards town.

EXT. SOUTHAMPTON MAIN STREET—DAY

Ted skulks down the sidewalk. He looks fairly battered, scratched, bloody. His feet are wet and he's missing a shoe. He's so intent on not getting spotted by Mrs. Vaughn that he passes right by Eddie and Ruth parking the Volvo without seeing them. Ted slips into a small bookstore.

INT. BOOKSTORE—DAY

Ted is peering out the window when MENDELSSOHN, the proprietor, touches his elbow.

> MENDELSSOHN
> Ted Cole!

> TED
> Yes. Good morning, Mendelssohn.

> MENDELSSOHN
> It's Ted Cole. It is, it is!

TED

Forgive me for bleeding.

MENDELSSOHN

Don't be silly. It's nothing you need be forgiven for.
Mendelssohn turns to a dumbstruck young woman on his staff.

MENDELSSOHN (CONT'D)

Bring Mr. Cole a chair. Can't you see he's bleeding?
The woman runs over with a chair. Ted seats himself. Mendelssohn grabs a pile of Ted's books and stacks them on a nearby desk, waiting for Ted's autograph.

TED

To put it simply, I need a ride home.

MENDELSSOHN

A ride? Yes, of course. You live in Sagaponack, don't you? I'll take you myself. Well . . . I'll have to call my wife. She may be shopping, but not for long. You see, my car is in the shop.

TED

I hope it's not in the same shop my car was in. I just got mine back from the shop. They forgot to reattach the steering column. It was like that cartoon—the steering wheel was in my hands, but it wasn't attached to the wheels.
Mendelssohn and the young woman are smiling and attentive. Ted gives the young woman the once-over. He thinks: Not really my type, sort of dull-looking but, that no-frills style usually means that they are open to "creative" experiences.

YOUNG WOMAN

I use a bicycle or else I'd take you home.

TED

Too bad.

EXT. VAUGHN HOUSE—DAY

Eduardo crawls out of the bush and half stumbles, half crawls over to the fountain. He splashes his face, only to realize that the water is brown and stinks like squid ink.

When he opens his eyes, Mrs. Vaughn is standing on the other side of the fountain holding a check.

MRS. VAUGHN

You warned him! You vile little man!
She picks up gravel from the drive and throws it at him.

MRS. VAUGHN (CONT'D)

You betrayed me!

EDUARDO

If you had killed him you would have gone to jail.

MRS. VAUGHN

Don't you want this? It's your last paycheck! You're fired!
Eduardo wipes his eyes.

MRS. VAUGHN (CONT'D)

Go fish!

She throws it into the fountain and storms off again. Eduardo wades into the fountain to retrieve it, but he's not surprised to see that the ink has run off, leaving it smudged and worthless.

Eduardo walks over to the bags of shredded drawings and shakes them out, spinning so that the wind picks them up and scatters them all over the yard, the privet, and beyond.

Drawing by Jeff Bridges

INT. FRAMESHOP–DAY

Eddie and Ruth stand at the counter. A salesgirl not much older than Eddie stands behind it, regarding Eddie with contempt.

SALESGIRL
Look—

EDDIE
No, *you* look. If there's no manager here, there must be someone else . . . there must be someone here besides you. I'm not leaving without that photograph.
The salesgirl scurries away into the back.

RUTH
Did you got mad at her?

EDDIE
Yes. I did.
From the back room we can hear the salesgirl describing the situation, and describing Eddie as scary. Scary? a voice asks. Eddie looks more confident than we've ever seen him, but he doesn't look scary. A handsome older woman appears, PENNY.

PENNY   (PLEASANTLY)
I understand that you're angry. I'm very sorry about that. When my customers are angry, I ask them to voice their complaints in writing, if you don't mind.

EDDIE
I work for Ted Cole. I'm a writer's assistant.

Then you won't mind writing, will you?

She pushes several sheets of paper and a pen towards him. Eddie looks at her for a moment, and then starts to write.

He writes: I have been sleeping with Mrs. Cole this summer. I esti-mate that we have made love sixty times.

Penny reads it.

PENNY (CONT'D)

Sixty times? Really?

Eddie nods and writes: Mr. Cole has had a mistress also. She was his model. Do you know Mrs. Vaughn?

PENNY (CONT'D)

The Vaughns on Gin Lane? We framed a painting for them called
The Epitome of Diabolism.
Eddie regards her, then writes: Okay.

PENNY (CONT'D)

Please go on.

Eddie writes: Okay. This morning Ted broke up with Mrs. Vaughn. Mrs. Vaughn was pretty upset about it. Meanwhile, Marion is packing up. She's leaving. Ted doesn't know she's leaving, but she is.

EDDIE

This is Ruth. She's four.
Ruth is playing with something.

PENNY

Yes, yes!

Penny leans over Eddie as he writes: Ruth doesn't know her mother is leaving, either. Both Ruth and her father are going to go back home and realize that Marion is gone. And all the photographs, every one of them, except the one you have here, in the shop.

PENNY (CONT'D)

Yes, my God—what?

Ruth scowls at Penny. Penny tries to smile at Ruth.

Eddie writes: Marion is taking the pictures with her. When Ruth goes home both her mother and all the pictures will be gone. Her dead brothers and her mother will be gone. And there's a story that goes with every picture, there are hundreds of stories, and Ruth knows them all by heart.

Eddie gives her a look.

PENNY (CONT'D)   (SHAKEN)

What do you want from me?

EDDIE

Just the photograph of Ruth's mother. She's in bed, in a hotel room, in Paris.

PENNY

Yes, I know the picture. Of course you can have it.

Eddie writes: Ruth needs to have something to put near her bed tonight.

PENNY (CONT'D)

But it's not a good picture of the boys—only their feet.

EDDIE

I know. Ruth likes the feet.

RUTH

Are the feet ready?

PENNY

Yes, they are, dear. I'll go check. It's almost ready, I'm sure.

Penny picks up the writing and the pen and starts to the back.

EDDIE

Excuse me, but could I have my writing back?

PENNY

Yes, of course.

She hands it back to him and goes to the back.

INT. BOOKSTORE—DAY

Ted is autographing away. His elaborate and beautiful signature would not look slight on The Declaration Of Independence.

A heavy-set, unappealing, middle-aged woman stands in front of Ted's table. He's signing for her.

WOMAN

It's really not out of my way.

TED

No, that's all right. Someone else will come along soon.

WOMAN

It's no trouble. I don't mind.

Ted thinks: I mind! Look at those mulish hips.

TED

No, really. Here you are.

He hands her the book with an insincere smile.

MENDELSSOHN

Most authors just scribble something illegible. Your signature is very, very beautiful.

TED

I really need a pen with a broader nib. Also some red ink—red
like blood, not like a fire engine.

MENDELSSOHN

Let me see.

INT. FRAMESHOP—LATER

*When Penny returns she has the picture and has obviously spruced herself up
a little bit; her hair is down, she has on fresh lipstick, and her shirt is unbuttoned a little more.*

PENNY

There's no charge for the photograph.

EDDIE

Thanks.

*He starts to go, but she grabs his wrist and puts before him something she has
written:* Is Marion Cole leaving you, too?

EDDIE (CONT'D)   (THIS HURTS)

Yes.

PENNY   (SOFTLY)

I'm sorry.

RUTH

Is the blood all gone?

PENNY

Yes, dear. It's as good as new.

Eddie picks Ruth up in one arm and the photograph in the other.

PENNY (CONT'D)

Young man, if you're ever interested in a job . . . .

Penny takes one of her business cards and puts it into Eddie's front pants pocket.

PENNY (CONT'D)

Perhaps next summer. I'm always looking for an extra
hand in the summer.

She smiles.

INT. BOOKSTORE–DAY

Two college-age girls stand in the corner. The pretty one, GLORIE, is watching Ted, shyly. The plain, heavy-set girl, EFFIE, seems bored. Ted looks at the pretty one appreciatively. He thinks: Aha!

EFFIE

She wrote her freshman English term paper on you.

GLORIE

Shut up, Effie.

TED

What was the title of your term paper?

GLORIE

An Analysis of the Atavistic Symbols of Fear in *The Door in the
Floor*. It's very tribal. You know, myths and fairy tales of tribal
peoples are full of images like magic doors and children
disappearing and people being so frightened their hair turns white
overnight. Primitive tribes have those fears.

Ted smiles and thinks: I'll show you something atavistic! I'll show you
something tribal!

And the snake, the snake is very tribal too, of course . . . .

TED

Of course. How long was this paper?

GLORIE

Twelve pages, not counting footnotes and a bibliography.
Ted laughs in her face, and then recovers with a smile.

TED

I don't suppose you girls have a car.
Believe it or not, I need a ride.
Effie rolls her eyes.

EXT. GIN LANE—DAY

Pieces of paper blow all over the street and across the neighborhood as Eduardo drives away in his truck.

EXT. FIRST NECK LANE—DAY

Ted and Glorie and Effie are walking to Glorie's house. Ted is flirting with Glorie, and Effie trails behind them rolling her eyes.

Ted spots Eduardo's truck and ducks behind a tree. Eduardo doesn't see him and just drives past.

INT. GLORIE'S HOUSE, KITCHEN—DAY

Ted is eating a sandwich. He is wearing different clothes. He is seated at the table with Glorie's mother, MRS. MOUNTSIER, an attractive widow. Glorie and Effie stand.

I'll get these clothes back to you right away.

MRS. MOUNTSIER

I was just going to give them to the Goodwill, anyway.
Bill was almost exactly your size.

Ted appraises her now. Mrs. Mountsier nervously plays with her wedding band. Glorie sits down and holds her mother's hand.

EXT. SOME YARD—DAY

Two boys are looking at a larger shred of paper, which depicts virtually all of Mrs. Vaughn's nude form.

INT. MASTER BEDROOM—DAY

The movers are carefully wrapping pictures of the boys. Marion is packing her clothes. One of the movers tapes up a package, gets to his feet, and goes over to a dresser where casually framed color snapshots of Ruth are arrayed.

MOVER

Are these pictures going also?

Marion goes over and picks one of them up. It is the picture that Eddie took of her and Ruth together. Ted has framed it. Marion's hands shake.

MOVER (CONT'D)

I could probably fit them all in one box.

Marion's eyes well up.

MARION

These aren't mine. These belong to my husband.

MOVER

Then I think we're pretty much done.

She doesn't respond until the guy leaves the room.

MARION

Okay.

She wipes her eyes, and regards herself in a small mirror hanging on the wall. Then she carefully puts the picture back in place. It's a happy image of a mother and daughter.

INT. MOUNTSIERS' CAR—DAY

Ted is seated in the front passenger seat. Mrs. Mountsier is driving, and the two girls are in the back. Ted is sort of half turned around, smiling.

TED

You know, it's a coincidence. I've been looking for two suitable subjects for a mother and daughter portrait—it's something I'm thinking about for my next book.

GLORIE

Wow! Do you want to do it, Mom?

TED

At first I would want to draw you and your daughter together. That way when I draw each of you separately, the presence of the other one is . . . somehow . . . there.

MRS. MOUNTSIER

How long would it take? And which one of us would you want to draw first separately?

TED

I should do Glorie first. First the two of you together, and then
Glorie alone, and then, when Glorie is back in college, you alone.
Big smile. Effie rolls her eyes again.

GLORIE

Mr. Cole, you're such a mystery to me. Which are you, an artist,
or a writer?

TED

I'm neither, Glorie. I'm just an entertainer of children. And I like
to draw.
*Smiles all around, except one. Mrs. Mountsier has turned onto Gin Lane.
Shreds of paper cling to the hedges and skitter across the road, but only Effie
notices.*

EFFIE

What is all this stuff?
Nobody pays attention to Effie.

MRS. MOUNTSIER

What sort of drawings do you have in mind?
*Ted smiles reassuringly, but is startled when a large fragment of paper lands
on the windshield with a loud SNAP. On it is a crudely sketched vagina.
Everyone in the car is startled; Glorie SCREAMS a little. The fragment
blows off, but many others blow around the car in a frenzy.*

TED

Don't stop! Use the windshield wipers!

EXT. BURGER STAND—DAY

Eddie and Ruth eat lunch at a picnic table. Alice isn't on shift.

EDDIE

Brave means you make the best out of what happens to you,
you just try to get over it.

RUTH

What about the cut?

EDDIE

In the whole rest of your life, whenever you need to feel brave,
just look at your scar. Your hand will grow bigger and your finger
will grow bigger but the scar will always stay the same size. And it
will always show up on your fingerprint.

RUTH

What's a fingerprint?

*Eddie takes Ruth's hand gently and dips her fingers in ketchup, then presses
them onto her paper plate.*

EDDIE

Those are your fingerprints. Nobody else will ever have
fingerprints like yours.

EXT. COLE DRIVEWAY—DAY

*Ted and the women pull up. Marion is just about to pull away. She looks pan-
icked for a minute, but then waits for him to climb out of the car. He comes
over to her window.*

*She is looking at him intensely, and this is the first time they have looked
each other in the eyes for a long time.*

*He leans in towards her. There seems to be something like a tender emo-
tion between them, but it turns into something else. She drives away.*

*He watches her leave, confused. The Mountsier ladies are looking at him.
He recovers with some small talk.*

INT. VOLVO–DAY

Eddie turns onto Parsonage Lane. The sunlight is slanted now. As Eddie drives up, the women are climbing in their car and pulling away. Ted looks at Eddie squarely, with restrained anger, but Eddie looks right back at him.

RUTH

Daddy, I got a scab. Show Daddy the scab.

Eddie takes the envelope out of the glove box as Ruth climbs out of the car, and then gets out himself. Ruth shows Ted the paper plate with the fingerprints on it.

RUTH (CONT'D)
Those are my fingerprints.

TED

That's really neat, Ruthie. So, you were at the doctor's getting the
stitches taken out?

RUTH

And we went to the beach, and had lunch, and Eddie showed me
my fingerprints.

TED

That's neat, Ruthie.

Eddie opens the trunk and takes the picture out. Now Ted seems almost wary.

TED (CONT'D)
I see the photograph was ready, finally.

RUTH
We got the feet back.

TED

You've got sand in your hair, Ruthie. You need a bath.

RUTH

No!

TED   (TO EDDIE)

Well, I waited quite a while for you this morning.

Where were you?

Eddie doesn't reply, but hands Ted the pages he wrote at the frame shop.

TED (CONT'D)

Where's Marion going?

EDDIE

I'll give Ruth a bath. Better read that.

TED

Answer me.

EDDIE

Read that first.

Eddie picks Ruth up and starts towards the house. Ted unfolds the crumpled
pages.

TED

What is this?

EDDIE

It's the only good writing I've done all summer.

Eddie and Ruth go in. Ted starts to read.

TED   (TO HIMSELF)

Sixty times?

He looks over his shoulder, then continues to read.

INT. UPSTAIRS HALLWAY—AFTERNOON

Ruth runs down the hallway, and Eddie chases after her. All the pictures are gone. The empty hooks stand out starkly.

INT. UPSTAIRS BATHROOM—AFTERNOON

Eddie hangs the picture of the feet back where it originally came from. He turns the tap on, then helps Ruth undress.

> RUTH (ALMOST WHISPERING)
> Did you saw that?
> *Eddie pulls her shirt over her head.*

> RUTH (CONT'D)
> Where are all the other pictures?

> EDDIE
> Maybe your Mommy moved them. Look at you—there's sand between your toes, in your hair, in your ears.

> RUTH
> It got in my crack, too.

> EDDIE
> It's a good time for a bath, all right!
> *Eddie lifts her into the tub.*

> RUTH
> But Mommy didn't move those things? What are those things?

EDDIE

Picture hooks.

INT. UPSTAIRS HALLWAY—AFTERNOON

Ted marches into the bathroom, pissed. But as soon as he opens the door, Eddie hands him Ruth, wrapped in a towel.

RUTH

Mommy moved all the pictures but not the—the—

TED

Picture hooks.

Ted hands Eddie his writing back.

RUTH

Why did she did that?

TED

I don't know, Ruthie.

EDDIE

I'm going to take a quick shower.

TED   (INTENSELY)

Make it quick.

INT. BATHROOM—SAME

Eddie closes the door, and leans against it. He lets out a long breath.

INT. HALLWAY—AFTERNOON

Eddie comes out of his room, washed and groomed, and walks towards the stairs. He clutches his screed in his hand. From down below we hear a woman's voice:

WOMAN   (OFF)

Hello? Hello?

From Ruth's bedroom:

RUTH   (OFF)

Mommy?

TED

Marion?

It's Alice. Eddie goes downstairs and meets her at the bottom.

EDDIE

Alice, there's a situation you should know about. Better read this.

Alice takes the pages, confused.

INT. TED'S WORKROOM—LATE AFTERNOON

Eddie sits on a sawhorse and waits. Ted holds a drink in one hand and dials a number on the wall phone with the other.

TED   (INTO PHONE)

Hi, it's Ted. I can't play today, Dave, my wife's left me. Yeah.

Okay.

Ted hangs up.

TED (CONT'D)

So where the fuck is she?

EDDIE

I don't know.

Ted SLAPS Eddie, hard.

TED

Don't lie to me!

Eddie recovers and PUNCHES Ted hard in the nose. Ted is hurt. They kind of WRESTLE around, knocking stuff over, and then break away from each other.

TED (CONT'D)

Jesus!

Ted holds his icy drink against his nose. He staggers around dizzily.

TED (CONT'D)

Christ! I hit you with my open hand! With the flat of my hand, and you make a fist and punch me in the nose!? Jesus!

EDDIE

Sorry. Marion said it would make you stop.

TED

"Marion said!" Christ, what else did Marion say?

EDDIE

I'm trying to tell you.

TED (SHOUTING)

If she thinks she's got a rat's ass of a chance to get custody of Ruth, she's got another thing coming!

EDDIE

She doesn't expect to get custody of Ruth.
Ted sits down, surprised.

EDDIE (CONT'D)

She has no intention of trying.

TED

She told you that?

EDDIE

She told me everything I'm telling you.
Ted leaps up.

TED   (SHOUTING AGAIN)

What kind of mother doesn't even try to get custody of her child?

EDDIE

She didn't tell me that.

TED

Okay . . . okay. Christ! Why did she have to take all the
photographs? There are negatives. She could have taken the
negatives and made her own photographs!

EDDIE

She took all the negatives, too.

TED

The hell she did!

*Ted runs over to the flat-file where the negatives used to be. The drawers are
empty.*

TED (CONT'D)

She can't have the photographs *and* the negatives. They were my
sons, too! I should have half the photographs, for Christ's sake.
What about Ruth? Shouldn't Ruth have half the pictures?

EDDIE

Marion said you'd say that, but she said no. I'm sure—the lawyer
will explain.

TED

Obviously she went to New York.

EDDIE

I doubt it.

TED

What the hell do you know? There's no other place she would go.
I even know where in the city she is.

EDDIE

I can't imagine her going to New York.

TED

You don't have an imagination, Eddie.
Ted sits down.

TED (CONT'D)

She's going to need money. What is she going to do for money?
Christ!

EDDIE

You were planning to get a divorce anyway, weren't you?

TED

Is that Marion's question, or yours?

EDDIE

Mine.

TED

Just stick to what Marion told you to say, Eddie.

EDDIE

She didn't tell me to get the photograph. That was Ruth's idea—
and mine.

TED

That was a good idea.

EDDIE

I was thinking of Ruth.

TED

I know you were. Thank you.

*They sit quietly for a moment. From the house they can hear Alice trying to
deal with Ruth. Ruth is apparently questioning her about the photographs,
and sounds shrill.*

RUTH   (OFF)

What about this one? Tell it!

ALICE   (OFF)

I'm sorry, Ruth. I don't know.

RUTH   (OFF—CROSSLY)

This is the one with Thomas in the tall hat. Timothy is trying to
reach Thomas's hat but he can't reach it because Thomas is
standing on a ball. Timothy got mad and started a fight.

ALICE   (OFF)

Was the fight in the picture?

RUTH (OFF — SCREAMING)

NO! The fight was after the picture!

Ted finishes his drink.

TED

You want a drink?

EDDIE

No thanks.

TED

What's tomorrow? Saturday?

EDDIE

Yeah.

TED

I want you out of here by tomorrow. Sunday at the latest.

EDDIE

I just need a ride to the ferry.

TED

Alice can take you.

INT. COLE KITCHEN — LATER

Alice is sitting in the kitchen. Apparently, she has been crying. She is upset,
almost hysterical. Eddie's writing lays on the table in front of her.

ALICE

She's asleep. She was crying.

Ted hands her his handkerchief.

TED

I'm sorry for springing all of this on you, Alice.

Alice is not appeased.

ALICE

Fuck you! My father left my mother when I was a little girl.
So I quit! That's all. I just quit!

She turns to Eddie.

ALICE (CONT'D)

And you should have the—the—the decency to quit, too!

EDDIE

It's too late for me to quit. I just got fired.

TED

I never knew you were such a superior person, Alice.

EDDIE

Alice has been superior to me all summer.

ALICE

I am morally superior to you, Eddie. I know that much!

Eddie looks chastened.

TED   (ARCHLY)

Morally superior. Now there's a concept! Don't you ever feel
morally superior, Eddie?

EDDIE

To you I do.

You see, Alice? Everyone feels morally superior to someone.

Alice picks up her bag and storms out, SLAMMING the door behind her.

EDDIE

There goes my ride to the ferry.

TED

You're a smart boy. You'll think of someone to give you a ride.

EDDIE

You're the one who's good at getting rides.

EXT. COLE HOUSE—EVENING

Alice climbs into Buzz-cut's car, and SLAMS the door. Buzz-cut PEELS out while throwing Ted and Eddie the bird. The colored sky, however, is beautiful.

INT. UPSTAIRS HALLWAY—NIGHT

Ted is holding Ruth, who has woken up again. They are doing the photographs quietly. The blank spots are silent.

INT. TED'S WORKROOM—NIGHT

Eddie is on the phone. It's fairly dark in here—light comes mostly from the adjacent kitchen.

EDDIE   (INTO PHONE)

Everything's fine, Dad. I didn't get fired. I just finished the job. I'll
wait for you in New London. At the pier.

Ted comes in and goes to the refrigerator for more ice.
Eddie finishes his call and hangs up.

EDDIE (CONT'D)

Is Ruth asleep?

TED

Finally. You want a drink?

Eddie shakes his head.

TED (CONT'D)

At least have a beer, for Christ sake.

Eddie accepts one. They wander out into the backyard.

EXT. BACKYARD—EVENING

There is still light in the sky, and light behind them in the house.

TED

Jesus, look at this yard. I can't believe she doesn't want custody of
her own daughter. What kind of mother leaves her daughter?

EDDIE

I don't know. I don't know her well enough to judge her.

TED

Let me tell you something, Eddie. I don't know her well enough
to judge her, either.

EDDIE

Don't forget, it's you she's really leaving. I guess she knew you
pretty well.

TED

Well enough to judge me? Oh, certainly!
Ted sucks on his ice cubes.

TED (CONT'D)

But she's leaving you, too, isn't she, Eddie? You don't expect her
to ring you up for a rendezvous, do you?

EDDIE

No, I don't expect to hear from her.

TED

Me neither.
Ted spits his cubes out.

TED (CONT'D)

Jesus, this drink tastes terrible.

EDDIE

I don't have a picture of her.

TED

I have drawings of her. I drew her. Long time ago. Before the
accident. She was so incredible. She was so . . . fucking . . .
beautiful and amazing. You should have known her then. She
hated to pose for me. Do you want to see?

EDDIE

Sure.
They go back inside.

INT. TED'S WORKROOM—EVENING

Ted goes over to his flat-file and turns on a work light. In one of the bottom drawers is a stack of sketches of Marion. They are good drawings and none of them are nudes.

TED

These are the only ones I kept.
Ted goes through them.

TED (CONT'D)

I was never good enough to draw Marion. I didn't know—
I didn't have the ability, I guess. In some of the
photographs you can see . . . .
Ted sips his drink and grimaces.

TED (CONT'D)

Do you want one? You can have one.
Eddie picks up one particularly good one. He really wants it, but he puts it back on the pile.

EDDIE

Ruth should have them.

TED

Good idea.

Ted looks softly at Marion's image, then sips his drink and grimaces. This time he looks at it in the light. It is black, and so is Ted's mouth. He spits out what's in his mouth.

EDDIE

Wrong cubes.

Ted GAGS and runs to the toilet. He's GAGGING and HEAVING.

Eddie looks at him for a moment and then exits, leaving Ted RETCH-
ING. The toilet bowl is filled with blackness.

DISSOLVE TO:

INT. EDDIE'S BEDROOM—NIGHT

The room is black, until the door opens a crack. Eddie wakes up as someone
draws the curtains closed, leaving only a trace of light on Eddie's face.

EDDIE   (SOFTLY)

Marion?

TED

Jesus . . . aren't you the optimist?

Eddie sits up and starts fumbling for the light. He turns it on, but Ted turns
it back off.

TED (CONT'D)

Forget the light, Eddie. This story is better in the dark.

EDDIE

What story?

TED

I know you want to hear it. You told me you asked Marion to tell
it to you, but Marion can't handle this story.

EDDIE

I remember.

Well, Thomas had his driver's license but Timothy did not.
Tommy was seventeen, he'd been driving for a year. Thomas was
a good driver. Alert and confident—he had excellent reflexes. And
Thomas was cynical enough to assume, as Ted had instructed him,
that every other driver is a bad driver. Who taught you to drive,
Eddie?

EDDIE

My dad.

TED

Good for him. Tell him for me that he did a good job.

EDDIE

Okay.

TED

We were out west. It was after a long day of skiing, and it had
snowed all day. A wet, heavy snow. A degree or two warmer and it
would have been rain.
At seventeen and fifteen respectively, Thomas and Timothy could
ski the pants off their parents, who often finished a day on the
slopes a trifle earlier than their boys.
That day, in fact, Ted and Marion had retired to the bar at the ski
resort, where they were waiting a long time for Thomas and
Timothy to finish their last run. And the last run after that.

EDDIE

You were drunk.

TED

That was one aspect of what would become trivial—in the area of
the ongoing argument between Ted and Marion, I mean. Marion
said that Ted was drunk, although in Ted's view he wasn't. And

Marion, while not drunk, had more to drink than she was accustomed to. Besides, Thomas had his driver's license and hadn't been drinking. There was no question as to who among them should be the driver.

EDDIE

So Thomas was driving?

TED

And brothers being brothers, Timothy sat beside him. Ted and Marion sat in the back seat, and they did what many parents do without cease; they kept arguing, though the nature of their arguments remained enduringly trivial. Ted, for example, had cleared the windshield of snow, but not the rear window. Marion argued that Ted should have cleared the rear window, too, but Ted countered that as soon as the car was warm and moving, the snow would slide off.

EXT. SKI RESORT PARKING LOT—DUSK

The Coles' rental car pulls out, and the snow does slide off the rear window. Night has fallen, and it is snowing.

We follow the car as it drives, and we hear Ted. We see the car for a little while and then tilt up to the dark and snowy sky, which dissolves back into the dark bedroom.

INT. EDDIE'S BEDROOM—NIGHT

TED

Ted and Marion began to quarrel about the best route to the hotel. It hardly helped Thomas as a driver that his mother

and father were determined to choose precisely
where he should turn left.

EDDIE

Okay, I see it.

TED

No, you don't see it. You can't possibly see it until it's over, Eddie.
Or do you want me to stop?

EDDIE

No. Don't stop.

EXT. SKI RESORT STRIP TOWN—NIGHT

Still snowing. We pick up the car moving down the strip.

TED

So, Thomas moves into the center lane—the turning lane, it's not
a passing lane—and Tommy puts on his blinker, not knowing that
both the lights are covered with wet, sticky snow that
his father had failed to clear off at the same time his father
failed to clear the rear window.
It is hard to see the car from behind.

INT. RENTAL CAR—NIGHT

MARION

Don't turn here, Tommy—it's safer up ahead, at the lights.

TED

You want him to make a U-turn and get a ticket, Marion?

I don't care if he gets a ticket. It's safer to turn at the lights.

THOMAS

Break it up, you two. I don't want to get a ticket, Mom.

MARION

Okay—so turn here then.
Thomas turns on the turn signal, which TICKS loudly.

TED

Better just do it, Tommy. Don't sit here.

TIMOTHY

Great back seat driving.
*Timmy notices that Tommy has turned his wheels. The TICKING of the turn
signal seems to grow louder and louder.*

TIMOTHY (CONT'D)

You cut your wheels too soon again.

THOMAS

It's because I thought I was going to turn and then
I thought I wasn't, asshole!

MARION

Tommy, don't call your brother an asshole, please.

TED

At least not in front of your mother.

MARION

No—that's not what I mean, Ted. I mean that he shouldn't call his
brother an asshole—period.

TIMOTHY

You hear that, asshole?

MARION

Timmy, please—

TED

You can turn after this snowplow.

THOMAS

Dad, I know. I'm the driver.

Suddenly the rear window is white with light and then there's an IMPACT.

EXT. SKI RESORT STRIP TOWN—NIGHT

The rental car, SMASHED from behind, is pushed right into the path of the oncoming snowplow, which virtually SLICES it in half.

INT. RENTAL CAR—NIGHT

We see what Ted describes and hear both his story and their dialogue.

TED   (V.O.)

Thomas was killed by the steering column. It crushed his chest. Tommy died instantly. And—for about twenty minutes—Ted was trapped in the back seat, behind Thomas. Ted couldn't see Thomas, although Ted knew Tommy was dead because Marion could see Tommy.

MARION   (DESTROYED)

Oh, Ted—Tommy's gone. Tommy's gone. Can you see Timmy? Timmy's not gone, too—is he? Can you see if he's gone?

EXT. TRAIN STATION PARKING LOT—NIGHT

Marion drags her wheeled suitcase across the uneven, gravelly parking lot towards the desolate train station. Marion stands on the empty platform, waiting. Close up on her face.

> TED (V.O.)
>
> Because Marion was trapped in the back seat behind Timothy—
> for more than half an hour—she couldn't see Timothy, who was
> directly in front of her. Ted, however, had a pretty good view of
> his younger son. But Ted couldn't see that the snowplow, as it cut
> the car in two, had also cut off Timmy's left leg at the thigh.

EXT. SKI RESORT STRIP TOWN—NIGHT

An ambulance and rescue crew struggle to disengage them all from the crumpled car. Sparks jump where somebody is CUTTING through metal, and red lights spin.

    Now Ted stands outside the car, Marion still stuck inside. The rescue workers free Timmy, and put his body on a stretcher and carry it away. One of his legs remains stuck, and most of his blood stays behind as well.

> MARION
>
> Timmy's not gone, too—is he? Can you see if he's gone?

> TED (V.O.)
>
> Timothy Cole bled to death from a severed femoral artery.
> *Marion is safely outside the car. Ted holds her, and supports her.*

TED (CONT'D) (V.O.)

Ted tried to tell her that her younger son, like her older son, was
dead. He just never managed to say it.

Marion spots Timmy's shoe sticking out of the wreckage.

MARION

Oh, look. He's going to need his shoe.

*Marion limps over to the car, and reaches down. We don't see the shoe or the
leg, but Marion's face.*

INT. EDDIE'S BEDROOM—NIGHT

TED

Ted wanted to stop her, but talk about turned to stone—I couldn't
move, I couldn't even speak. And so Ted allowed his wife to
discover that her son's shoe was still attached—to his leg. That
was when Marion realized that Timothy was gone, too. And
that—that is the end of the story.

INT. EDDIE'S BEDROOM—NIGHT

*Ted gets up and opens one curtain to let in the dead, gray, pre-dawn light. His
mouth is still black.*

TED

It was after Ruth was born before Marion said anything to me. I
mean she hadn't said a word—not one word. But one day, Marion
walked into my workroom and said to me: "How could you?" And
we never talked about it again. I tried, but she just wouldn't talk
about it. I hired you, Eddie, because you look like Thomas.
I knew that Marion would fuck you. I gave her you.

Drawing by Jeff Bridges

EDDIE

Get out.

TED

Just don't think that you know me, or Marion. You don't know
us—you don't know Marion, especially. You knew her shadow,
you knew a fragment of Marion. Before the accident, she was ten
times more than what you had. I had the best of Marion.

EDDIE

Please get out of here.
Ted heads towards the door.

TED

See you in the morning, Eddie.
Ted leaves. Eddie lays there with his eyes wide open.

EXT. TRAIN STATION PLATFORM—PRE-DAWN

Marion waits as the train pulls into the station. She climbs on. It pulls away.

EXT. COLE HOUSE—MORNING

A pick-up truck is IDLING in the driveway.

INT. COLE KITCHEN—MORNING

Eddie enters to see Ted peering warily out the window.

TED

It's Eduardo. What is Eduardo doing here?

EDDIE

Maybe Mrs. Vaughn hired him to kill you.

Ted ducks out of sight, and Eddie approaches the window.

TED

No, not Eduardo! But do you see *her* anywhere? She's not in the
cab, or in the back?

EDDIE

Maybe she's lying down under the truck.

Ted tries to see if she's there, then turns and scowls at Eddie.

TED

I'm being serious, for Christ's sake.

EDDIE

So am I.

TED

Why don't you go find out what he wants?

EDDIE

Not me. I've been fired.

TED

For Christ's sake—at least come with me then.
I can't go out there alone.

EDDIE

I better stay by the phone. If he has a gun and shoots you,
I'll call the police.

*Through the kitchen window, Eddie watches as Ted comes out of the house
cautiously, carrying a sleepy Ruth. Eduardo climbs out of his truck. Eduardo
holds his smeared check from Mrs. Vaughn in his hand. They talk.*

EXT. COLE HOUSE—MORNING

Ted and Eduardo converse. Ruth, straddling Ted's hip, listens quietly.

TED

Let me be sure I understand you, Eduardo. You think that you saved my life and that this cost you your job.

EDUARDO

I did save your life. It did cost me my job.

TED

Well, Eduardo, I play squash regularly and I'm pretty fleet of foot, but I do appreciate your brave warning. How much money are we talking about, exactly?

EDUARDO

I'm not here for a handout. I was hoping you might have some work for me.

TED

You want a job?

EDUARDO

Only if you have one for me.
They regard the neglected landscaping.

EDUARDO (CONT'D)

It doesn't look like you have a job for me.

TED

Just wait a minute. Let me show you where I want to put a pool.

INT. COLE KITCHEN—MORNING

Eddie watches them walk around the house, Ted talking animatedly.

EXT. COLE BACKYARD—MORNING

Ted is discussing the landscaping plan with Eduardo. Ted seems energized.
Eddie approaches them.

TED

And I want more lawn. I want a lawn like an athletic field.

EDUARDO

You want lines painted on it?

TED

No, no. I want a lawn the *size* of an athletic field.

EDUARDO

That's a lot of lawn. A lot of mowing. A lot of sprinkling.

TED

Whatever you say. I'm putting you in charge.
What about your wife?

EDUARDO

What about her?

TED

Well, does she work? What does she do?

EDUARDO

She cooks. She looks after our grandchildren—and some other
people's children too. She cleans some people's houses.

TED

Maybe she'd like to clean this house. Maybe she'd like to cook for
me, and look after my daughter, Ruth.

EDUARDO

Hello, Ruth.
Ruth hides her eyes, shyly.

EDUARDO (CONT'D)

I'll ask her. I bet she'll want to do it.

TED

So, when can you start?

EDUARDO

Whenever you want.

TED

Well, you can start today, Eduardo. You can begin by driving this
boy to Orient Point.

EDUARDO

Sure, I can do that.

TED

Eddie, you can leave immediately. I mean before breakfast.

EDDIE

That's fine with me. I'll go get my things.
Eddie heads into the house.

INT. EDDIE'S BEDROOM—MORNING

Eddie is packing his stuff hurriedly. At the bottom of his duffel bag he finds Marion's pink cashmere cardigan and her lilac silk matching camisole and panties set. Eddie sits down and holds them to his face.

EXT. COLE DRIVEWAY—DAY

Eddie sits in the passenger side of Eduardo's truck. Ted stands there.

TED

Well, you're a good driver, Eddie.
Ted holds out his hand. After a moment, Eddie shakes it.

TED (CONT'D)

About Marion—there's another thing you should know. Even before the accident, I mean even if there had never been an accident, Marion would still be difficult. Do you understand what I'm saying, Eddie?

EDDIE

I don't believe it.
Ted steps away. Eduardo pulls back slowly.

TED

About the shoe . . . it was a basketball shoe, an Air Jordan I think he called it.
Eddie looks at Ted, appalled.

TED (CONT'D)

Specific details, Eddie. Specific details.
Ted waves. Eduardo pulls out.

INT. EDUARDO'S TRUCK—DAY

They are driving along, listening to a little MUSIC. Eddie pulls his scribbled writing from the frame shop out of his pocket.

EDUARDO

Anyhow, what's it like working for Mr. Cole?
Eddie thinks for a long moment, then tries and fails to be flippant.

EDDIE

It had its perks.
Eduardo nods sagely.

EDUARDO

You were his assistant?

EDDIE

Yeah.

EDUARDO

What did you assist him with?
Eddie looks sideways at Eduardo. They drive on.

EXT. UPPER DECK OF THE FERRY—DAY

Eddie sits in the lee of a bulkhead, practicing Ted's elaborate signature on a scrap of paper. He has his family copy of The Mouse Crawling Between the Walls *next to him. He looks up at the horizon, and then signs the cover-leaf:* Dear Minty and Dorothy, Marion and I both loved having your son with us this summer; he's welcome back anytime. Su Amigo, Ted.
Eddie smiles to himself.

INT. SQUASH BARN—DAY

Ted is practicing by himself, playing incredibly hard, SMASHING the ball faster and faster until he can't keep up with it. Then he retrieves it and starts again, almost possessed.

EXT. BOW OF THE FERRY—DAY

The ferry approaches the New London docks. Eddie stands at the rail. He can see his parents waiting for him on shore. They spot him and are smiling and hugging each other, tears of joy in their eyes. Eddie can't help but smile to see them.

EXT. NEW LONDON TRAIN STATION—DAY

Adjacent to the docks is the train station parking lot; this is where Eddie's parents parked. As Eddie and his parents walk to their car, Minty and Dorothy babbling excitedly at Eddie, Eddie notices Marion's tomato-red Mercedes parked in the lot. Written in the dust on the trunk are the words: Not so fast, Abernathy.

Eddie looks around quickly, as if Marion might be nearby. He sees the empty train platform, realizes that she is gone, and walks with his parents to their car. Eddie goes instinctively to the driver's door, but his father gives him a look. Eddie remembers where he is and climbs into the back seat.

EXT. COLE BACKYARD—DAY

Eduardo is hosing down some newly planted shrubs. Ruth is behind him. They're playing with the hose and laughing.

INT. HALLWAY—DAY

*The window at the end of the hallway is open, and the sound of Ruth's laugh-
ter carries in from the yard. On the long bare hallway walls, only one photograph is hanging—the one from the hotel in Paris, the one with the feet.*

INT. PARIS HOTEL ROOM—FLASHBACK—MORNING

*It's early in the morning, and sunlight streams in the window. Ted and his
young sons enter with breakfast and wake Marion, who is beautiful, sleepy,
laughing, and happy in a way that we haven't seen yet. The boys, 5 and 7,
jump on the bed and goof around. Ted starts taking pictures as the boys dis-
appear under the covers. CLICK, CLICK, CLICK. The frame advance noise
dominates but fades into the gentle rhythm of a train.*

INT. SQUASH BARN—LATER

*The noise of the ball SLAMMING against the wall continues over this shot
even though Ted is now still, laying as if crucified on the red line T.*

*Ted opens the hatch in the floor and climbs down the ladder, pulling it
closed behind him. The court is empty.*

FADE TO BLACK

TOD CULPAN WILLIAMS, also known as Kip, is the writer and director of *The Door in the Floor* (This Is That, Revere and Focus Features), starring Kim Basinger and Jeff Bridges, and based on the novel *A Widow for One Year* by John Irving.

Kip grew up in New York City with his mother, a dancer, and his father, an architect. He studied painting and literature at Bard College and Columbia University. Later, he worked as a stringer for the *New York Times* Los Angeles bureau before attending the American Film Institute. In 1997 he wrote and directed *The Adventures of Sebastian Cole* (Paramount Classics), which premiered internationally at the Toronto Film Festival, was selected for main competition at the Sundance Film Festival, and earned nominations for two IFP Independent Spirit Awards (Best Supporting Actor and Best Screenplay).

Kip lives in New York City and Alden, Michigan.